Pea, Bee, & Jay

LIFT OFF

Brian "Smitty" Smith

HARPER alley

An Imprint of HarperCollinsPublishers

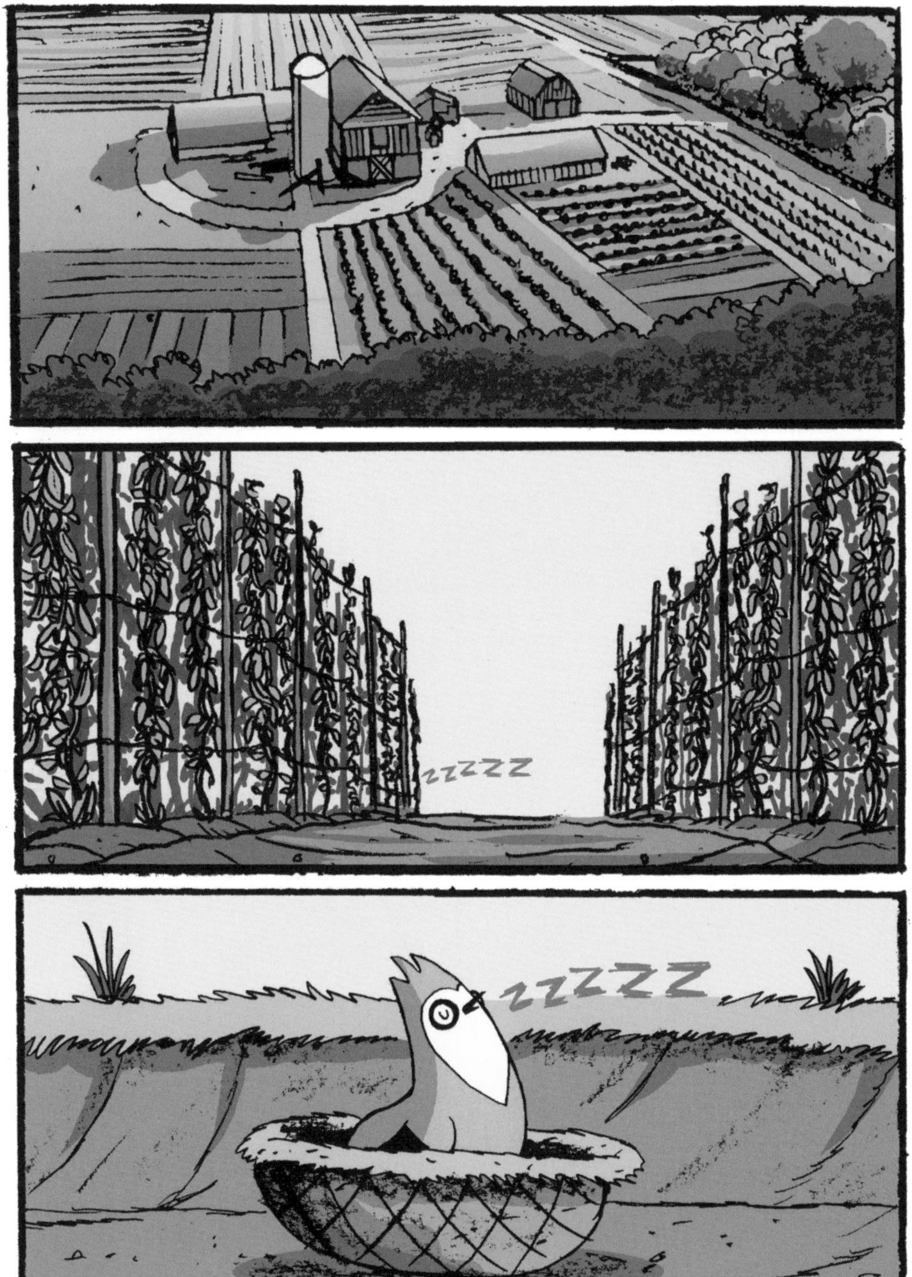
zzzzz
zzZZZ

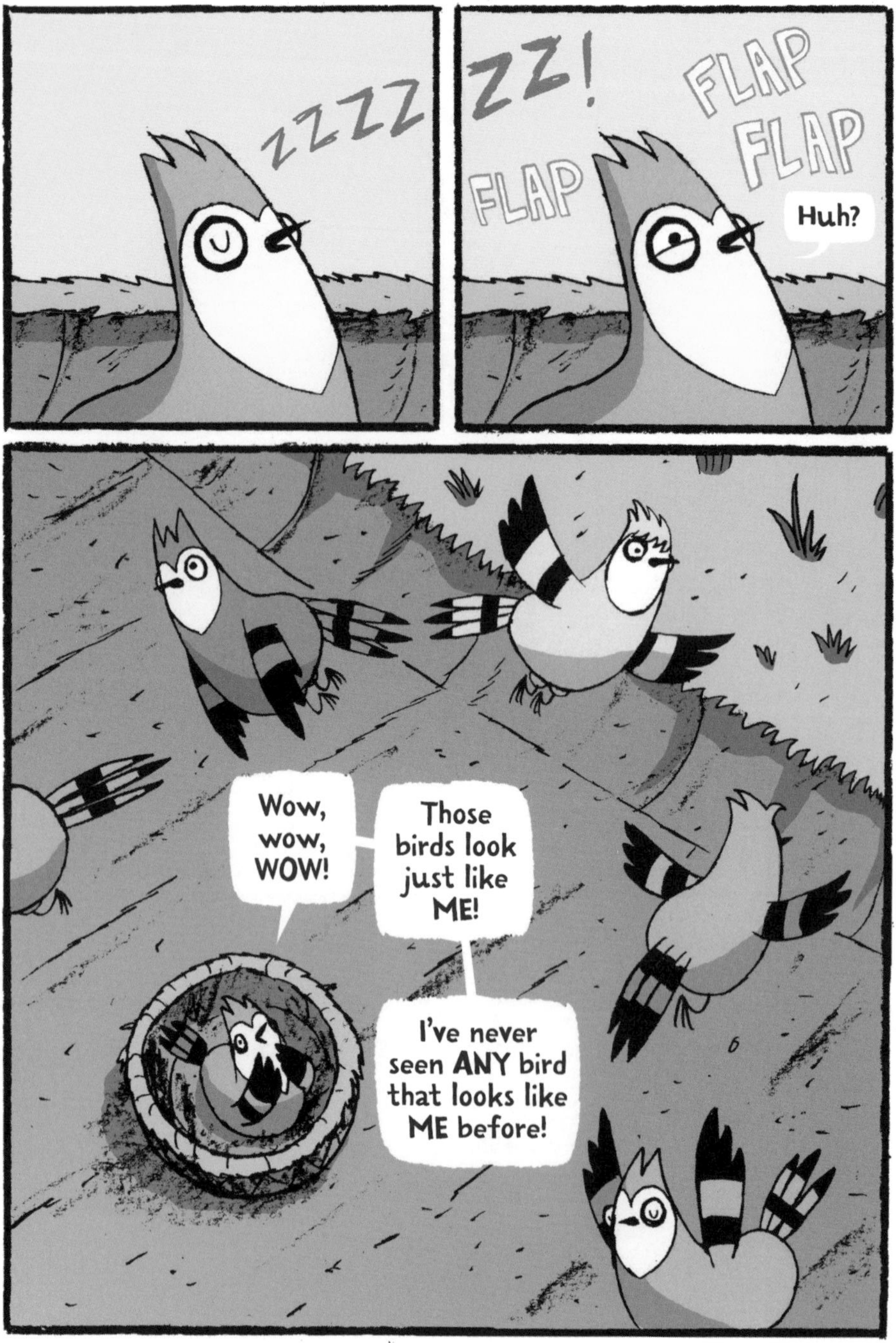
ZZZZZ
ZZ!
FLAP
FLAP
FLAP
Huh?
Wow, wow, WOW!
Those birds look just like ME!
I've never seen ANY bird that looks like ME before!

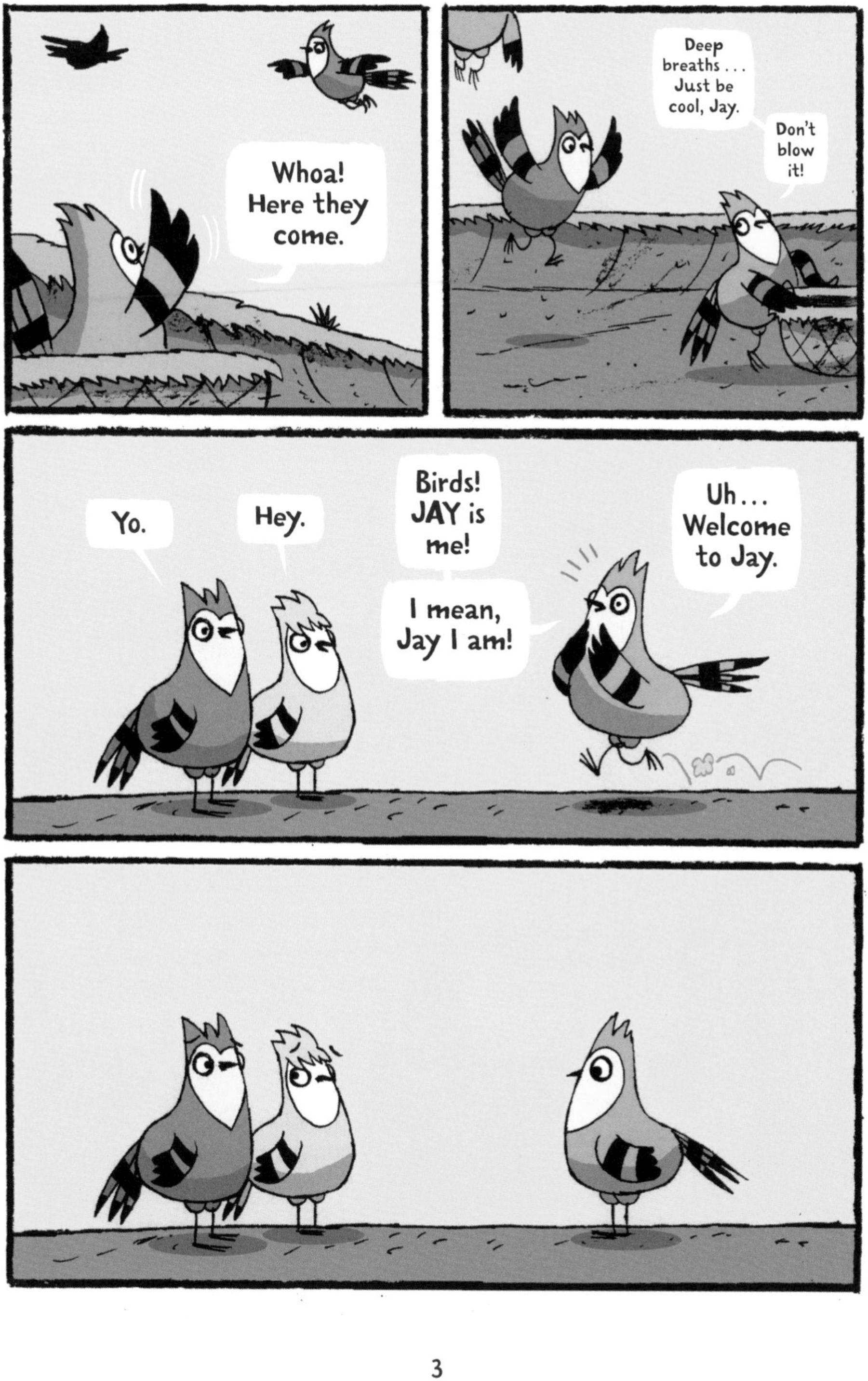
Whoa! Here they come.
Deep breaths . . . Just be cool, Jay.
Don't blow it!
Yo.
Hey.
Birds! JAY is me!
I mean, Jay I am!
Uh . . . Welcome to Jay.

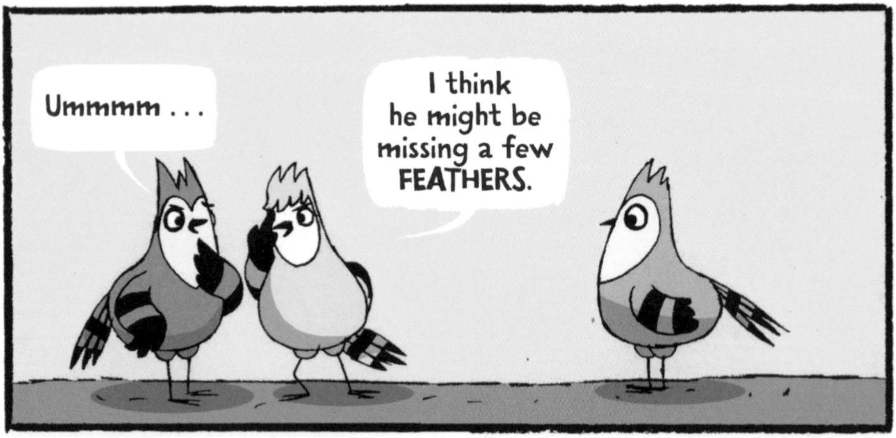
Ummmm . . .
I think he might be missing a few FEATHERS.

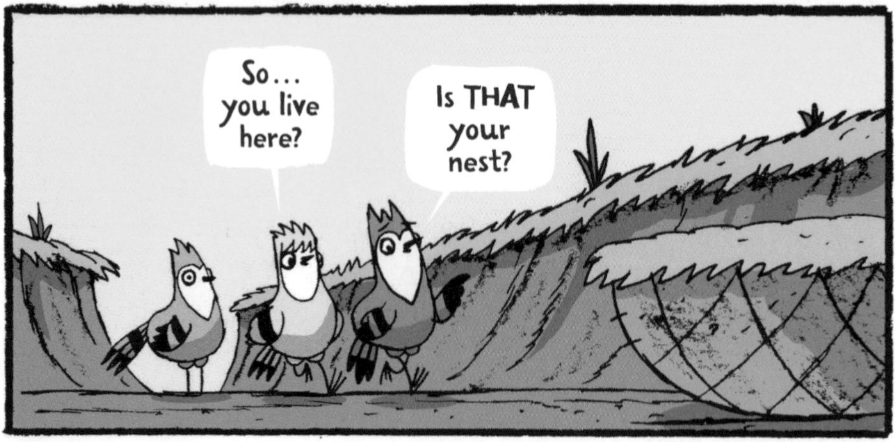
So… you live here?
Is THAT your nest?

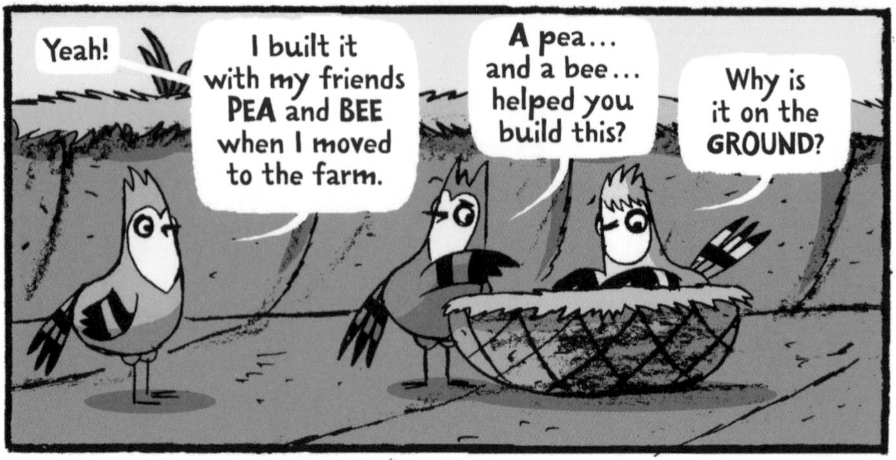
Yeah!
I built it with my friends PEA and BEE when I moved to the farm.
A pea… and a bee… helped you build this?
Why is it on the GROUND?

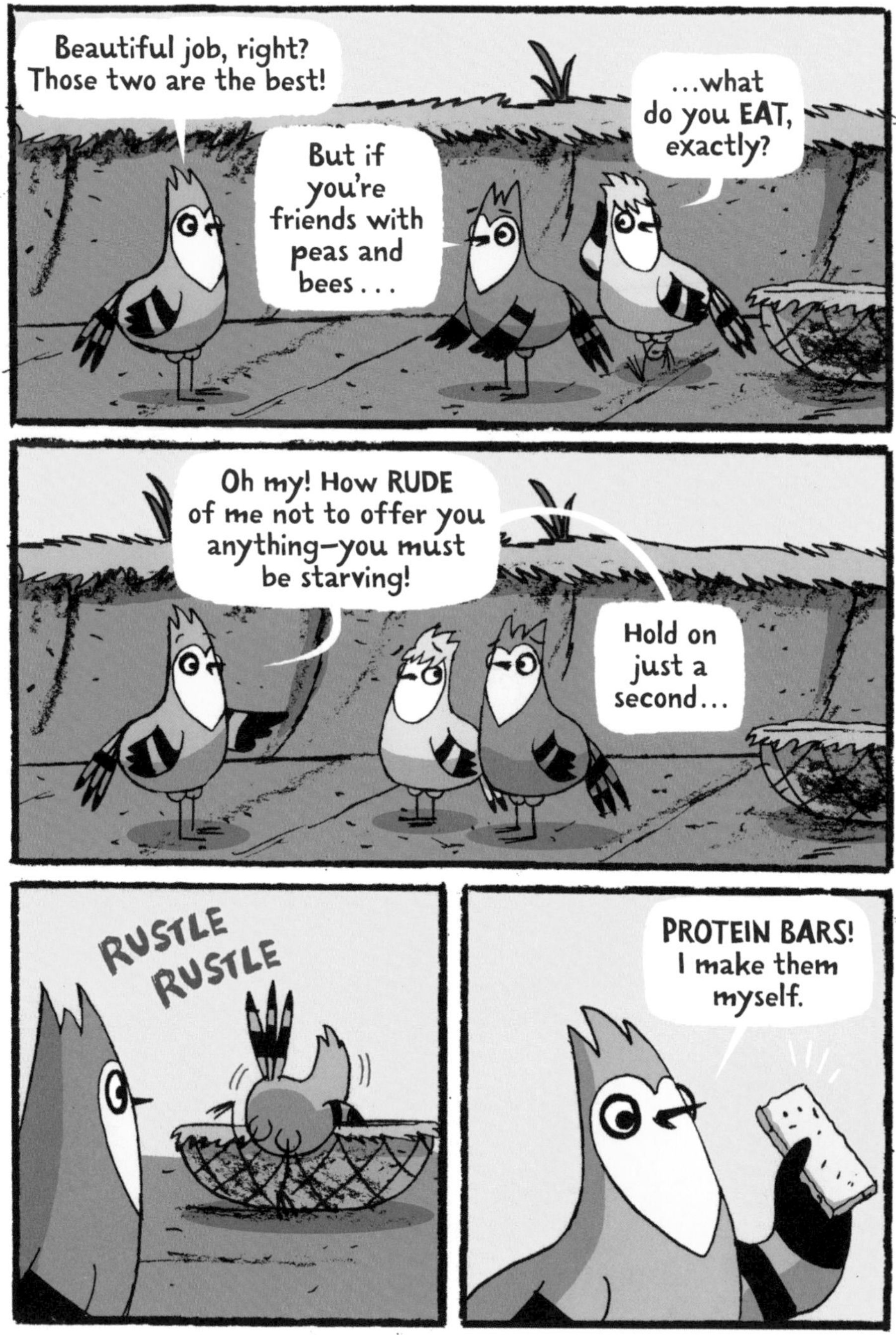
Beautiful job, right? Those two are the best!
But if you're friends with peas and bees . . .
. . . what do you EAT, exactly?
Oh my! How RUDE of me not to offer you anything—you must be starving!
Hold on just a second . . .
RUSTLE RUSTLE
PROTEIN BARS! I make them myself.

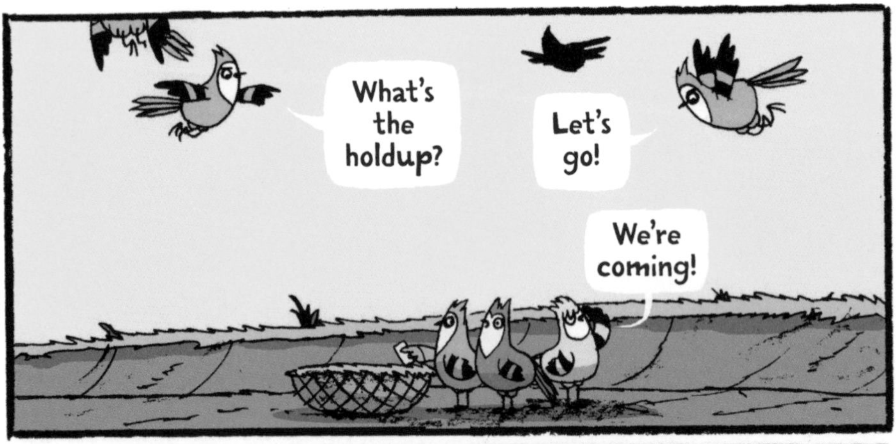
What's the holdup?
Let's go!
We're coming!

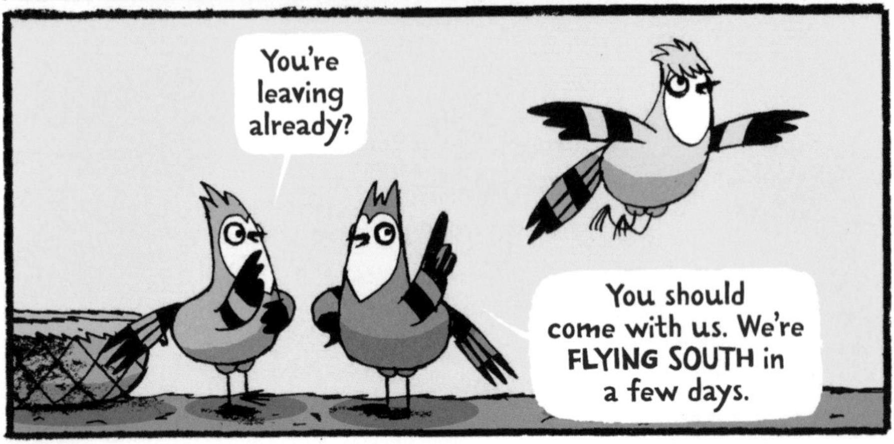
You're leaving already?
You should come with us. We're FLYING SOUTH in a few days.

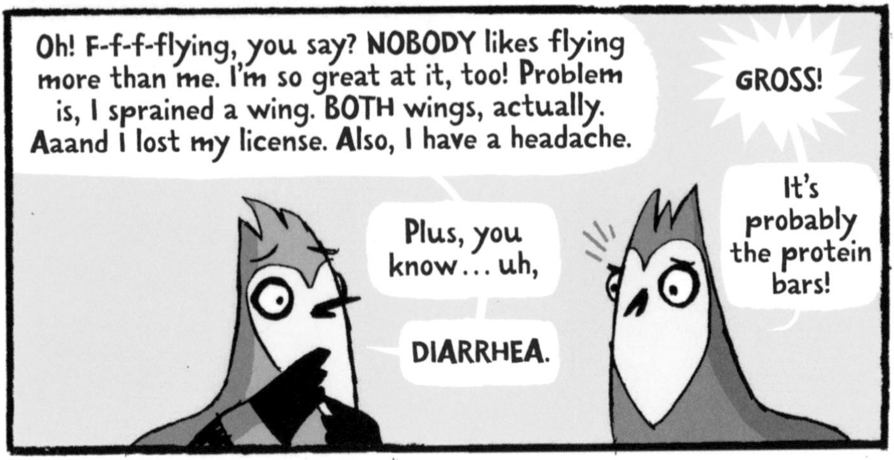
Oh! F-f-f-flying, you say? NOBODY likes flying more than me. I'm so great at it, too! Problem is, I sprained a wing. BOTH wings, actually. Aaand I lost my license. Also, I have a headache.
GROSS!
Plus, you know… uh,
DIARRHEA.
It's probably the protein bars!

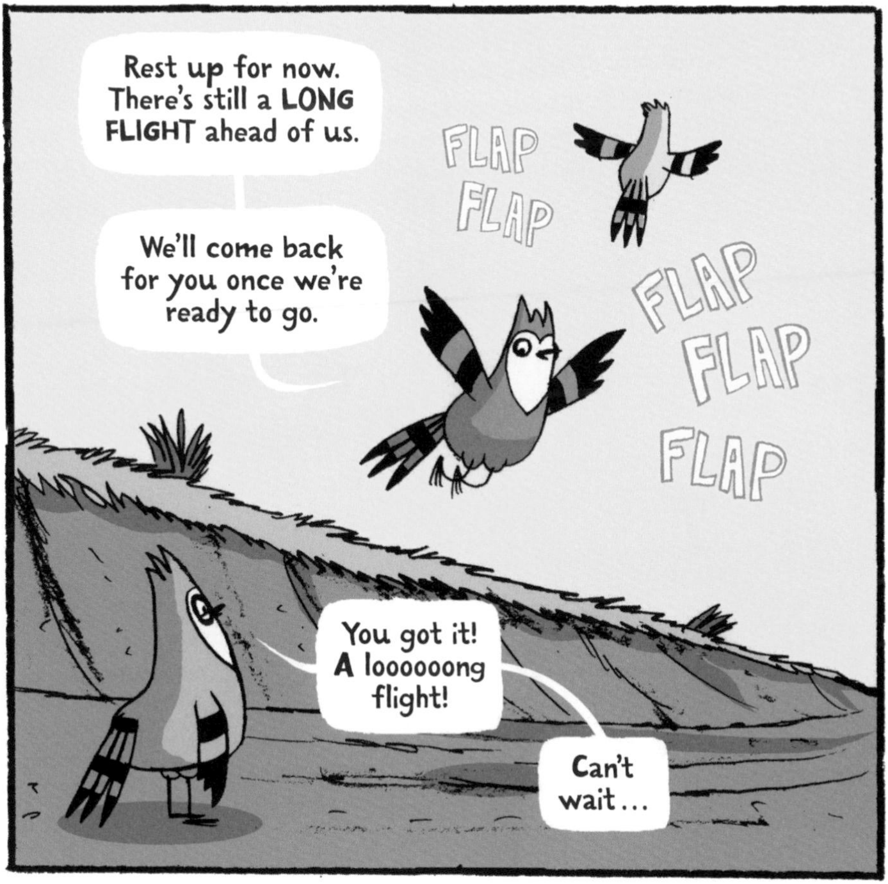
Rest up for now. There's still a LONG FLIGHT ahead of us.
We'll come back for you once we're ready to go.
FLAP FLAP
FLAP FLAP FLAP
You got it! A loooooong flight!
Can't wait...

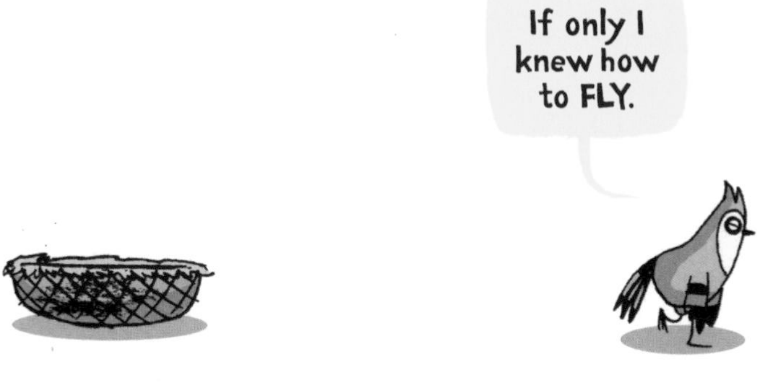
If only I knew how to FLY.

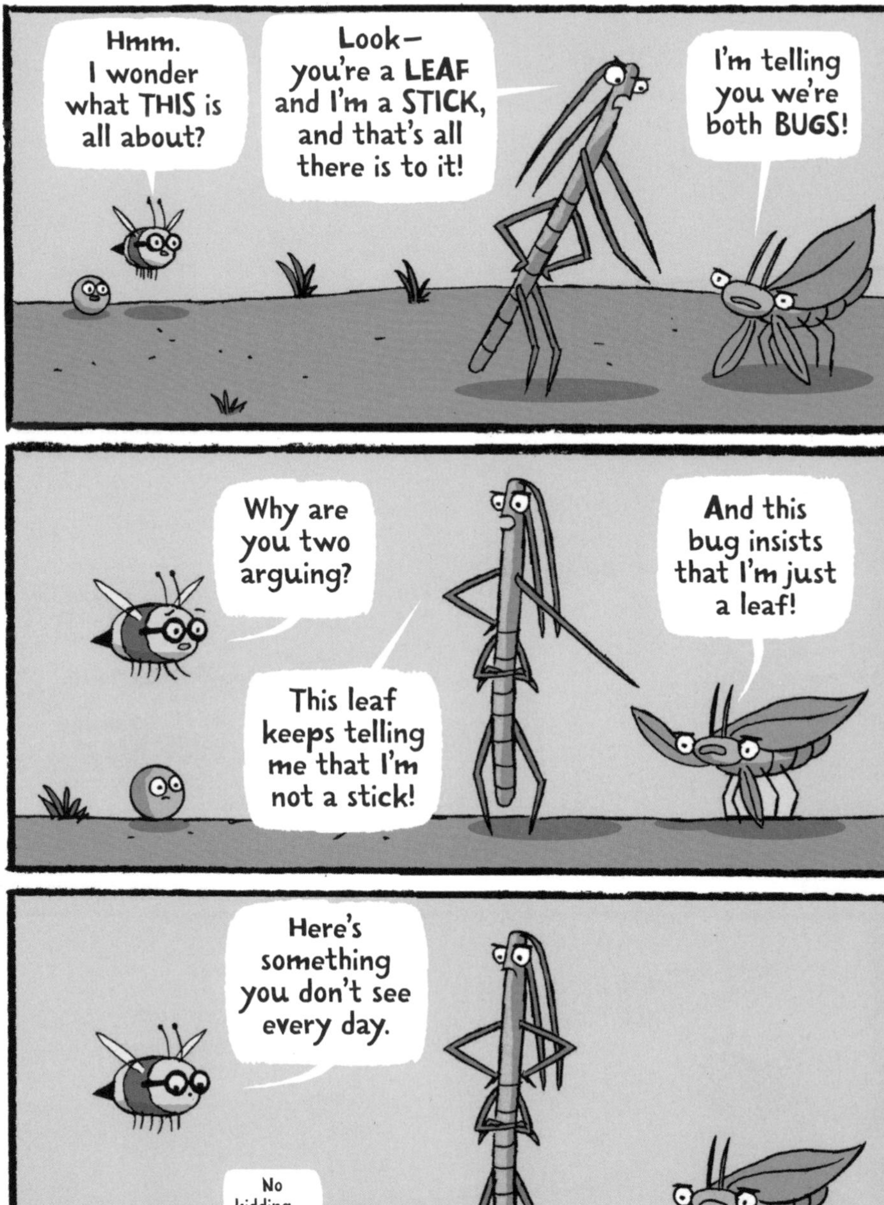
Hmm. I wonder what THIS is all about?
Look— you're a LEAF and I'm a STICK, and that's all there is to it!
I'm telling you we're both BUGS!
Why are you two arguing?
This leaf keeps telling me that I'm not a stick!
And this bug insists that I'm just a leaf!
Here's something you don't see every day.
No kidding...

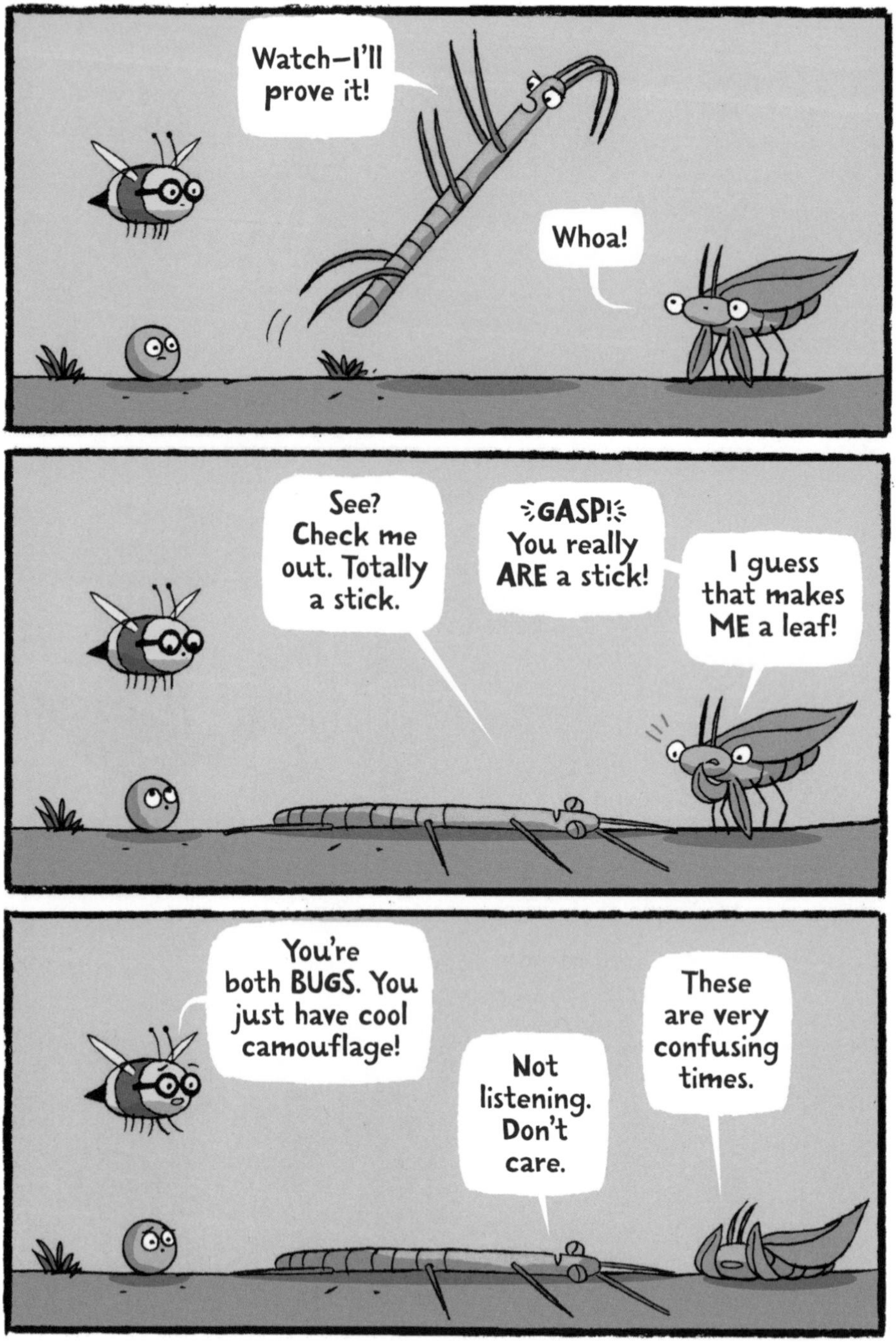
Watch—I'll prove it!
Whoa!
See? Check me out. Totally a stick.
GASP! You really ARE a stick!
I guess that makes ME a leaf!
You're both BUGS. You just have cool camouflage!
Not listening. Don't care.
These are very confusing times.

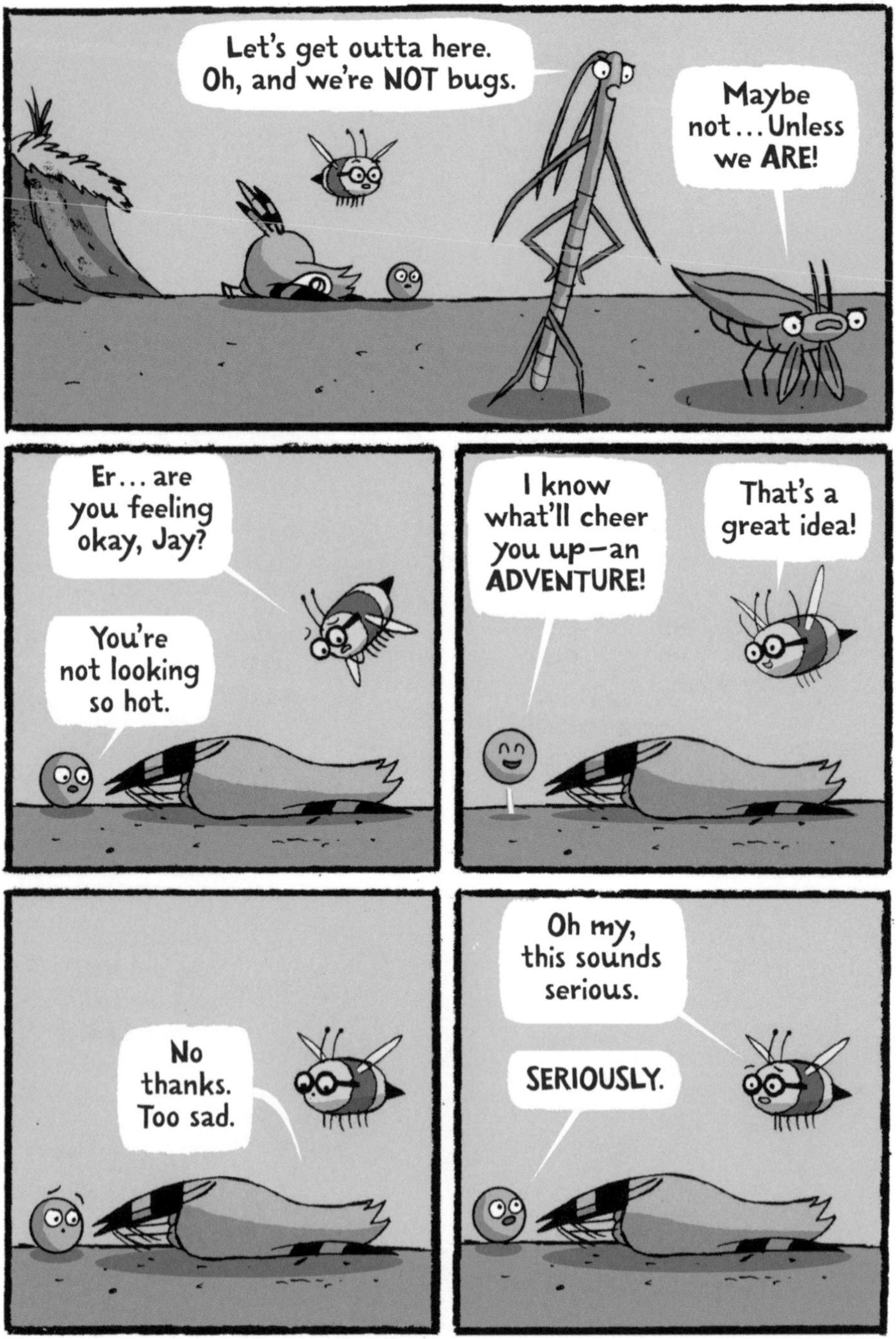
Let's get outta here. Oh, and we're NOT bugs.
Maybe not... Unless we ARE!
Er... are you feeling okay, Jay?
You're not looking so hot.
I know what'll cheer you up—an ADVENTURE!
That's a great idea!
No thanks. Too sad.
Oh my, this sounds serious.
SERIOUSLY.

*IT HAPPENED IN BOOK #1!

16

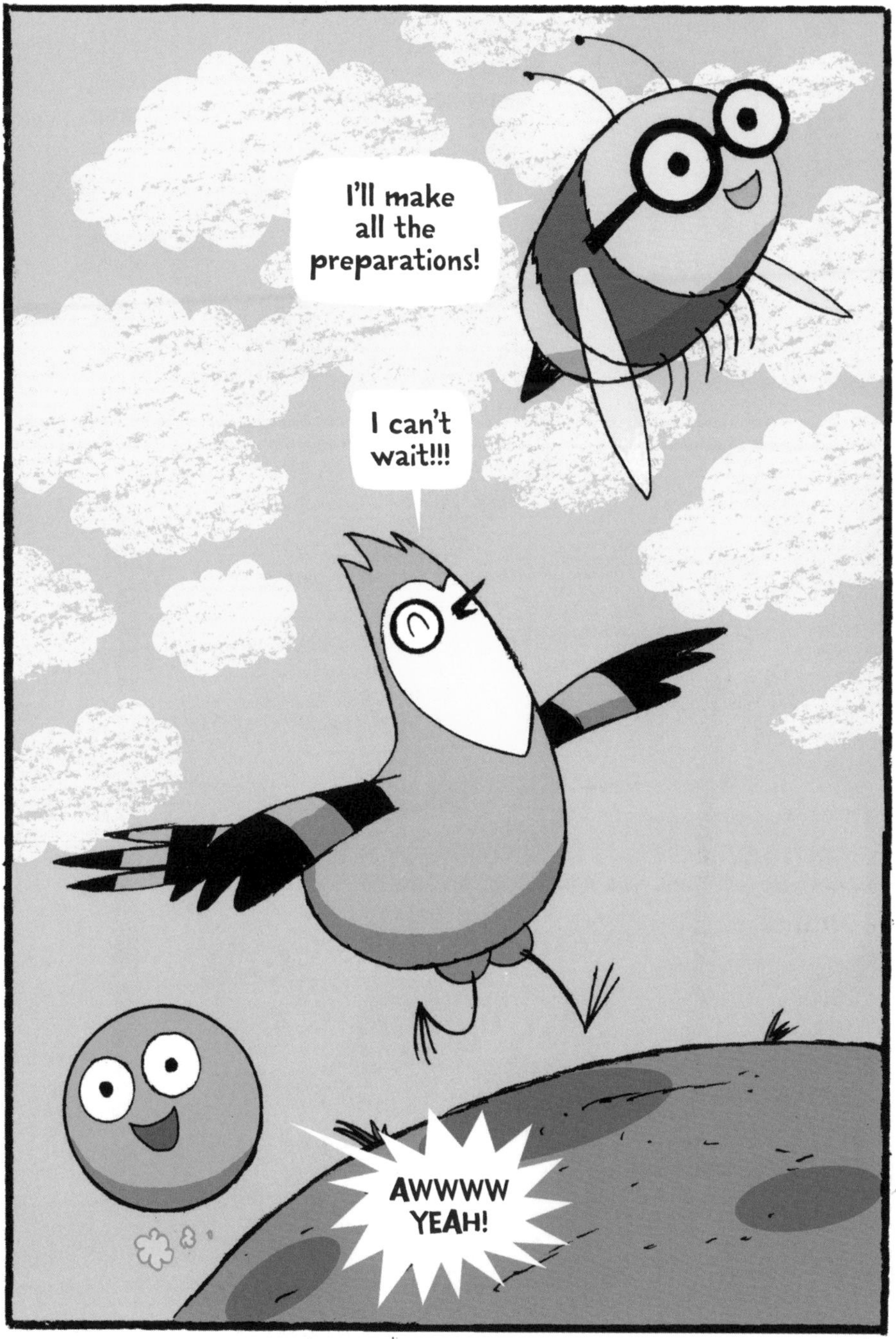
I'll make all the preparations!
I can't wait!!!
AWWWW YEAH!

18

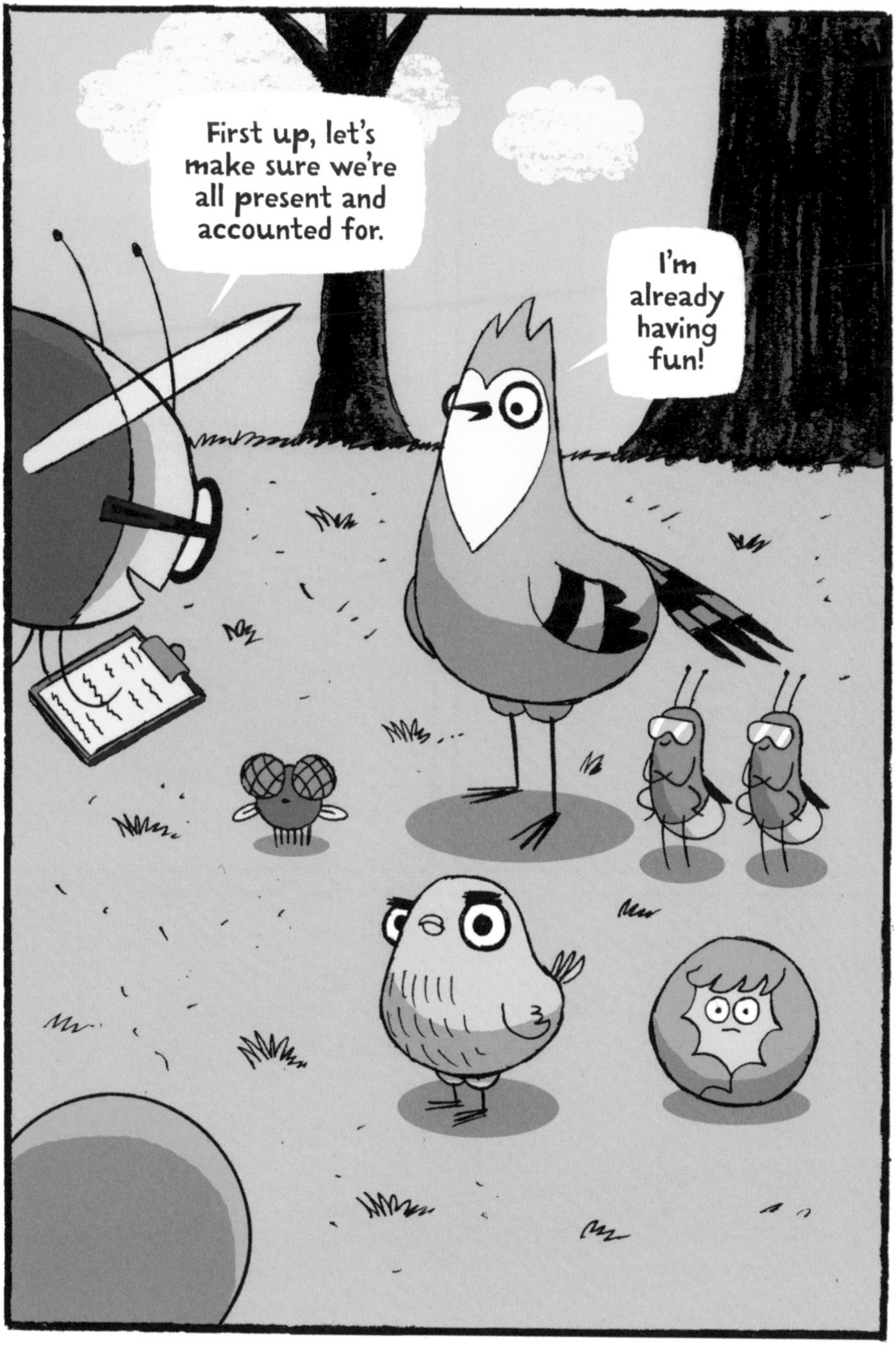
First up, let's make sure we're all present and accounted for.
I'm already having fun!

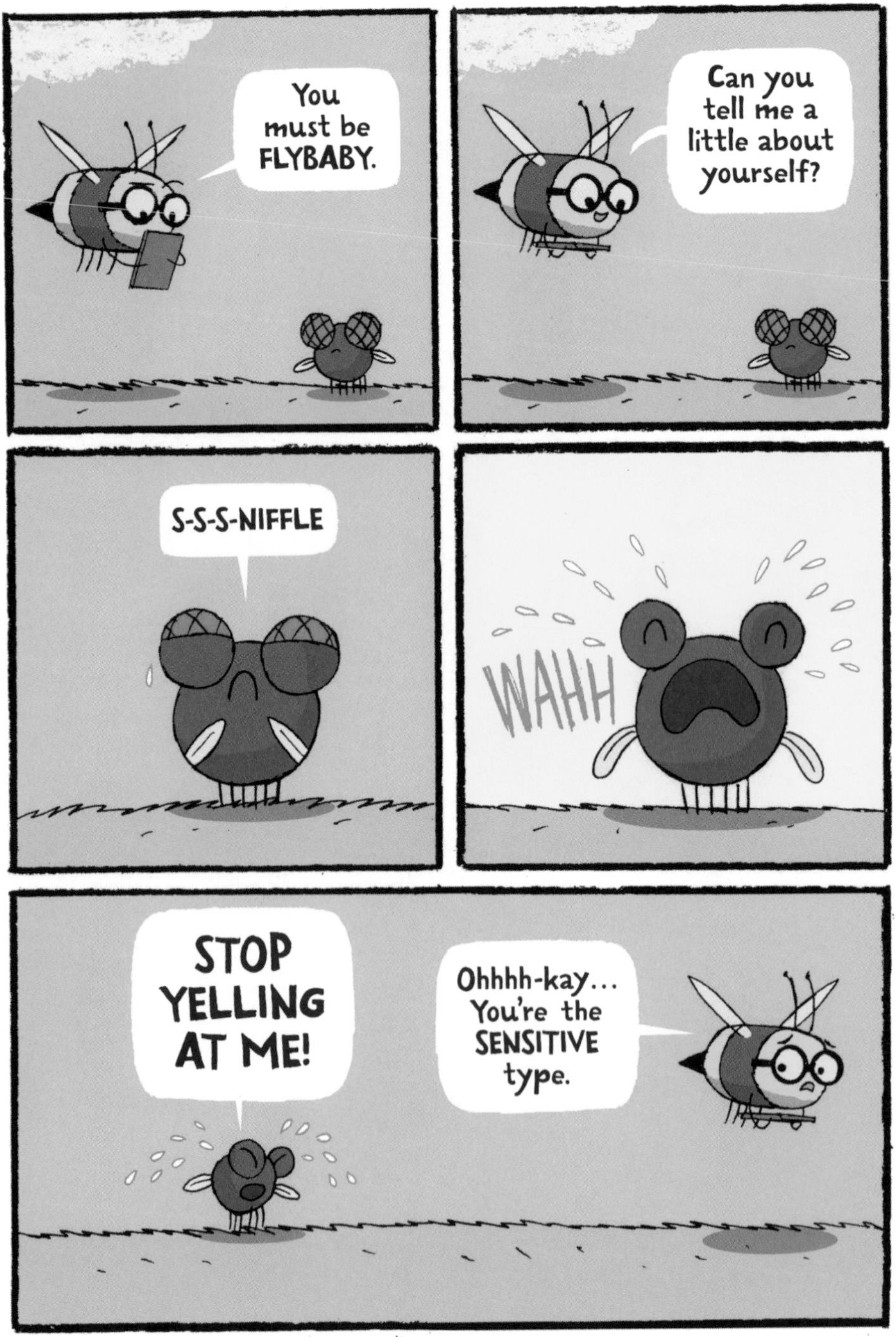
You must be FLYBABY.
Can you tell me a little about yourself?
S-S-S-NIFFLE
WAHH
STOP YELLING AT ME!
Ohhhh-kay... You're the SENSITIVE type.

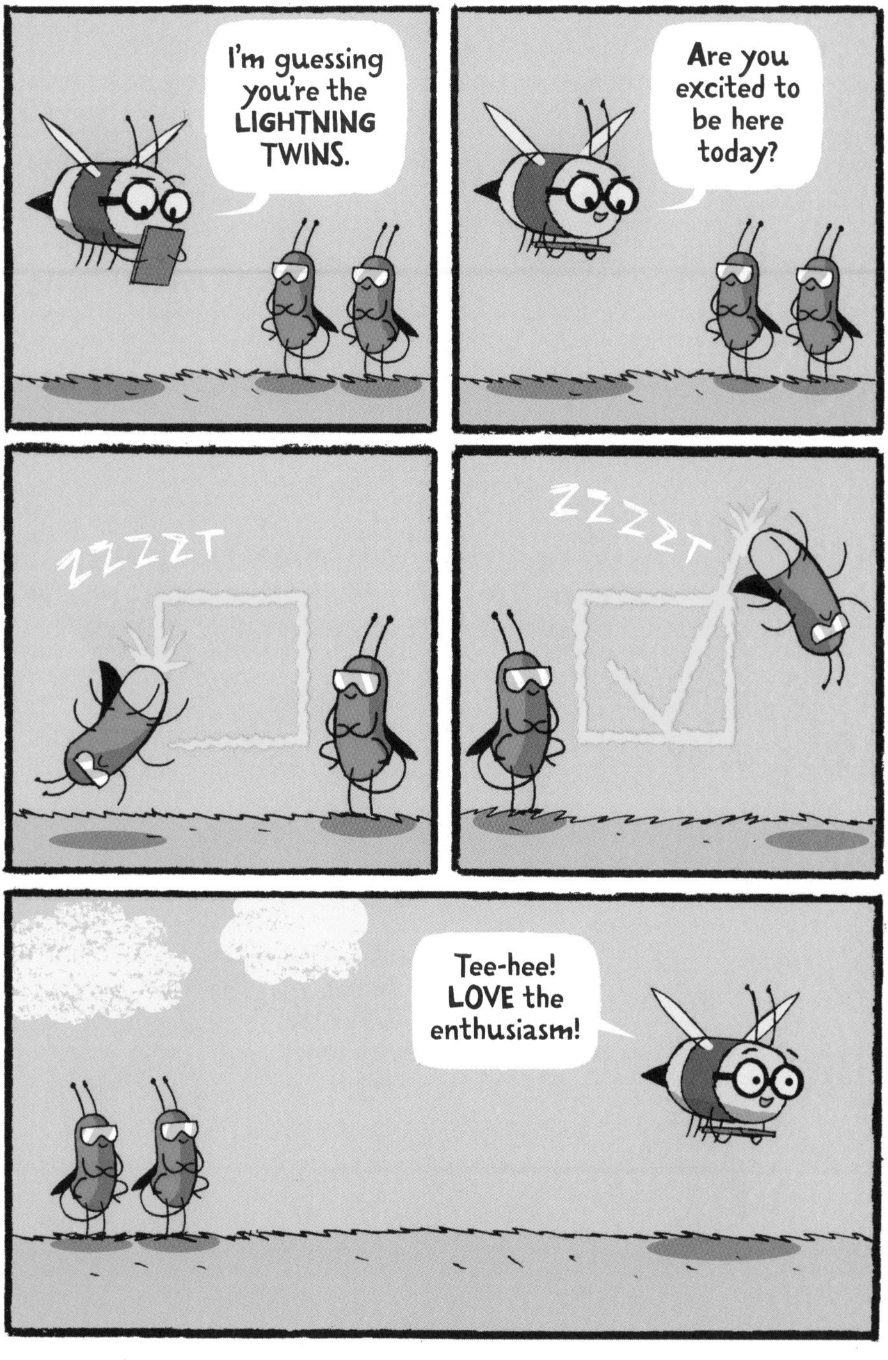
I'm guessing you're the LIGHTNING TWINS.
Are you excited to be here today?
ZZZZT
ZZZZT
Tee-hee! LOVE the enthusiasm!

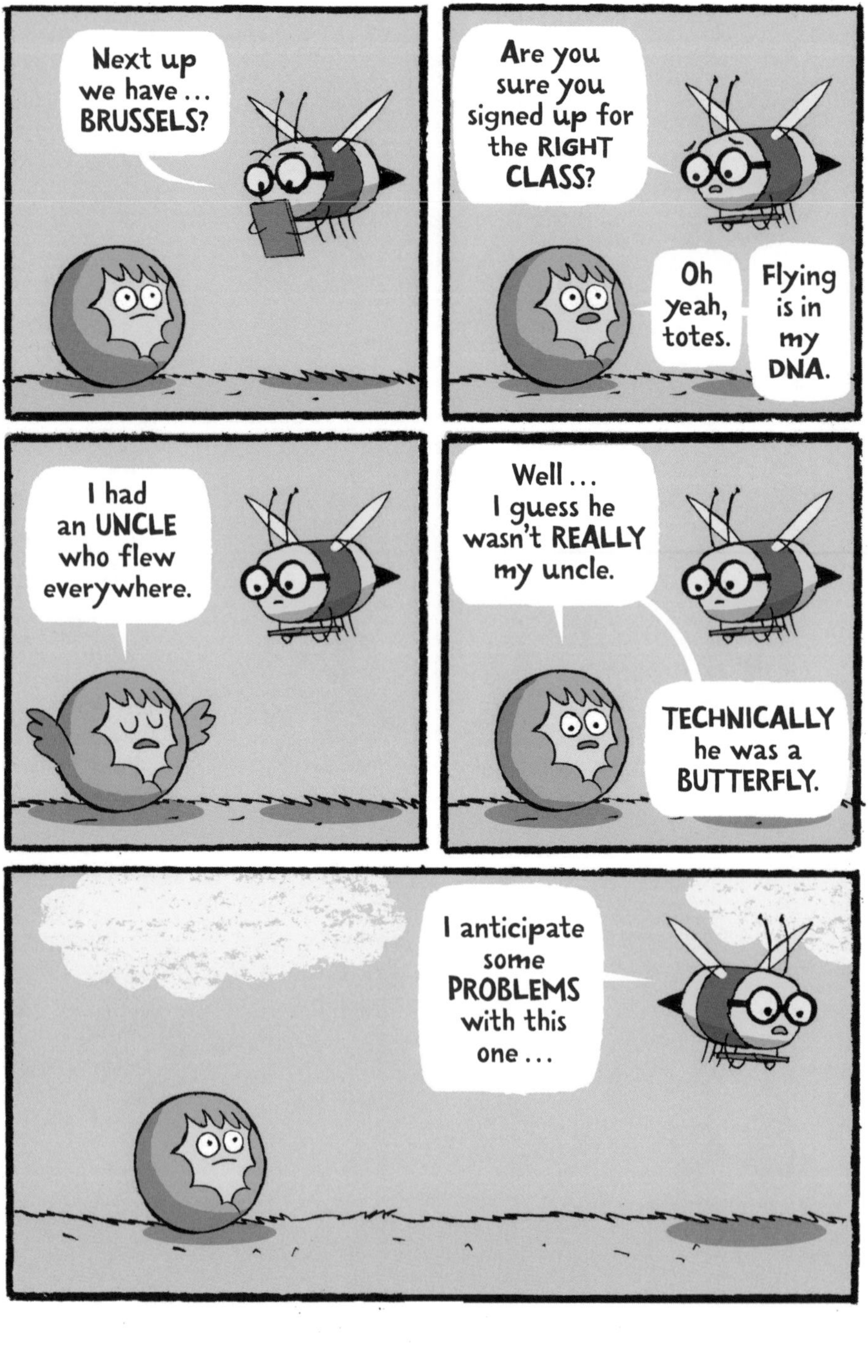

Next up we have … BRUSSELS?
Are you sure you signed up for the RIGHT CLASS?
Oh yeah, totes.
Flying is in my DNA.
I had an UNCLE who flew everywhere.
Well … I guess he wasn't REALLY my uncle.
TECHNICALLY he was a BUTTERFLY.
I anticipate some PROBLEMS with this one …

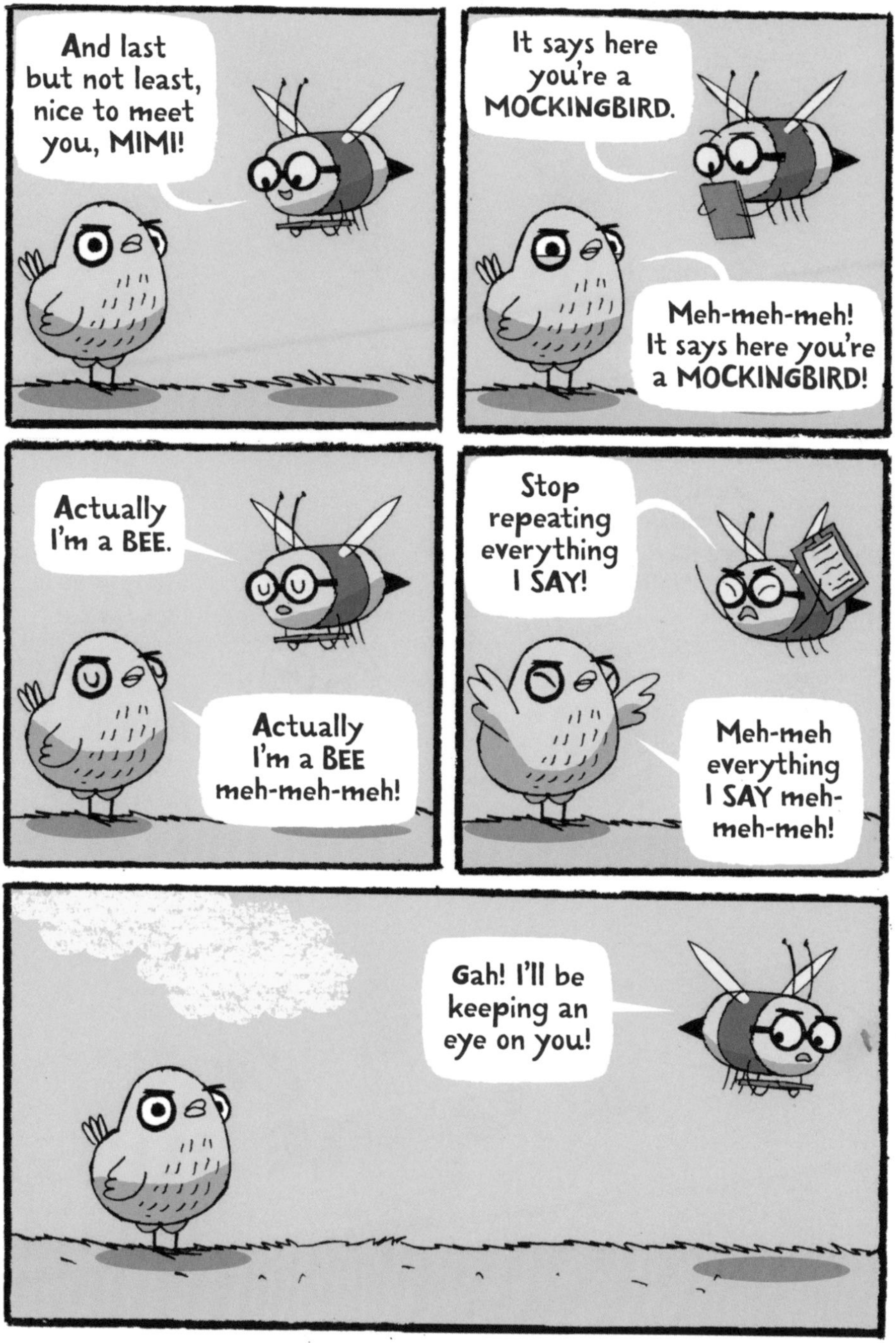
And last but not least, nice to meet you, MIMI!
It says here you're a MOCKINGBIRD.
Meh-meh-meh! It says here you're a MOCKINGBIRD!
Actually I'm a BEE.
Actually I'm a BEE meh-meh-meh!
Stop repeating everything I SAY!
Meh-meh everything I SAY meh-meh-meh!
Gah! I'll be keeping an eye on you!

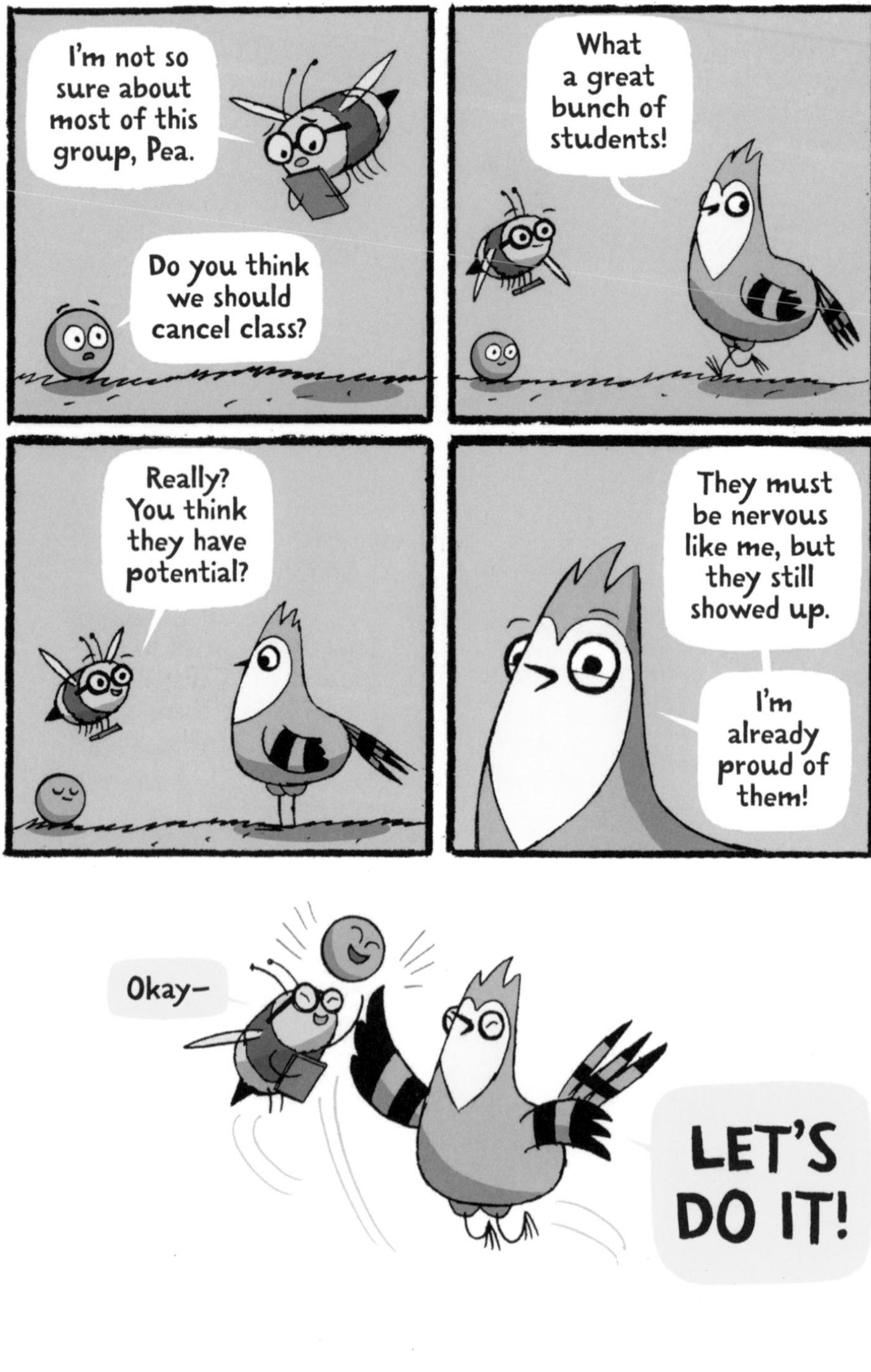
I'm not so sure about most of this group, Pea.
Do you think we should cancel class?
What a great bunch of students!
Really? You think they have potential?
They must be nervous like me, but they still showed up.
I'm already proud of them!
Okay–
LET'S DO IT!

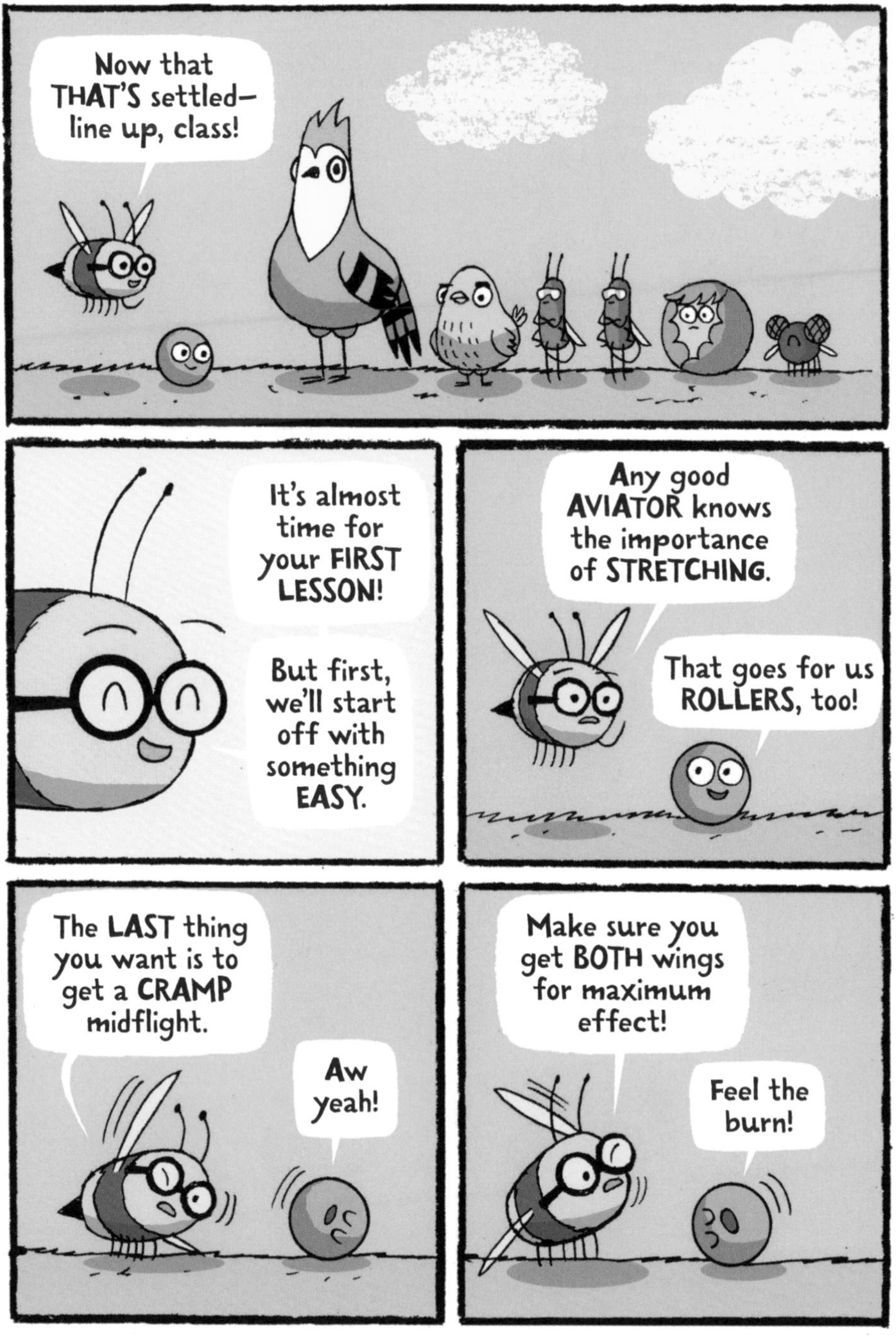
Now that THAT'S settled– line up, class!
It's almost time for your FIRST LESSON!
But first, we'll start off with something EASY.
Any good AVIATOR knows the importance of STRETCHING.
That goes for us ROLLERS, too!
The LAST thing you want is to get a CRAMP midflight.
Aw yeah!
Make sure you get BOTH wings for maximum effect!
Feel the burn!

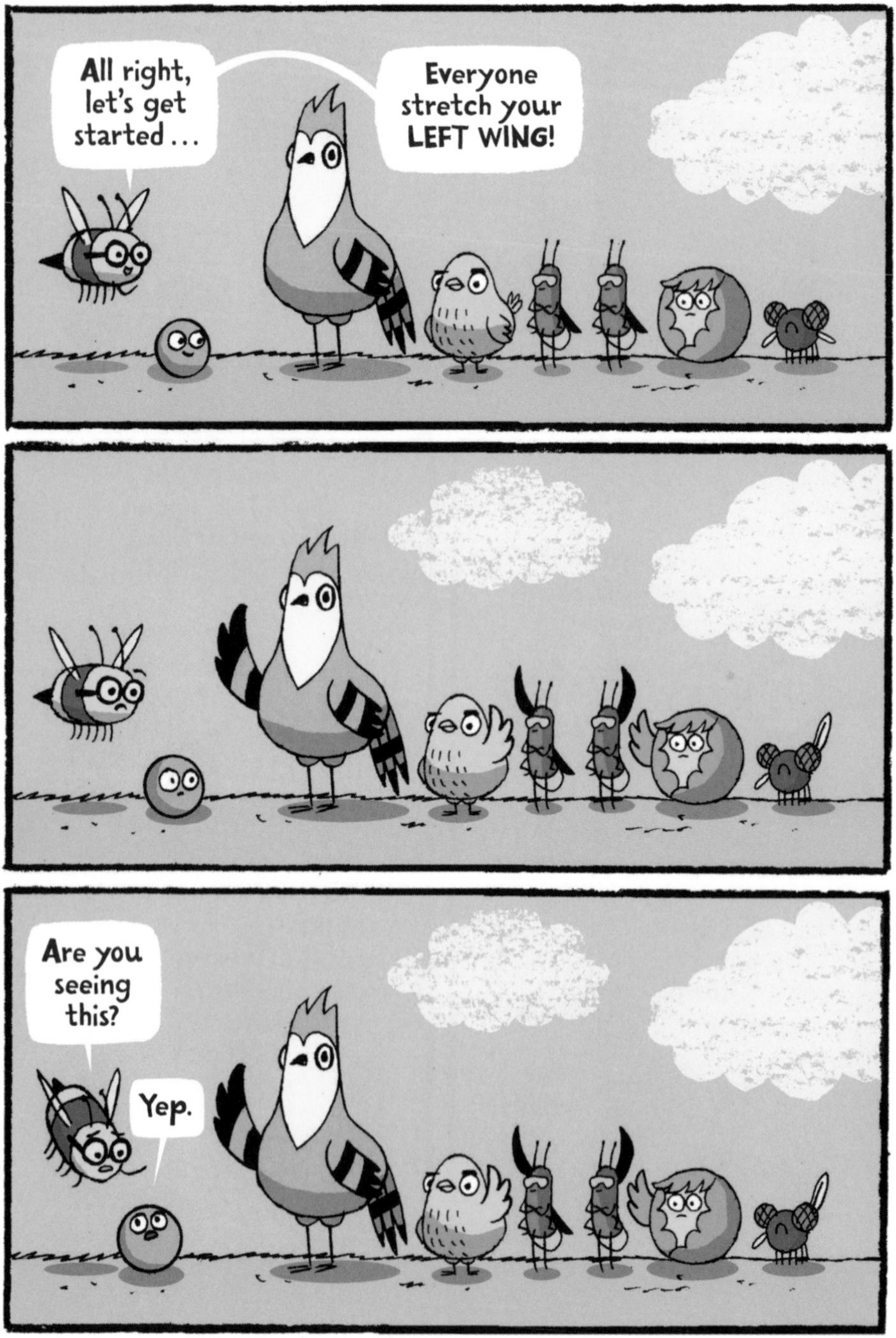
All right, let's get started...
Everyone stretch your LEFT WING!
Are you seeing this?
Yep.

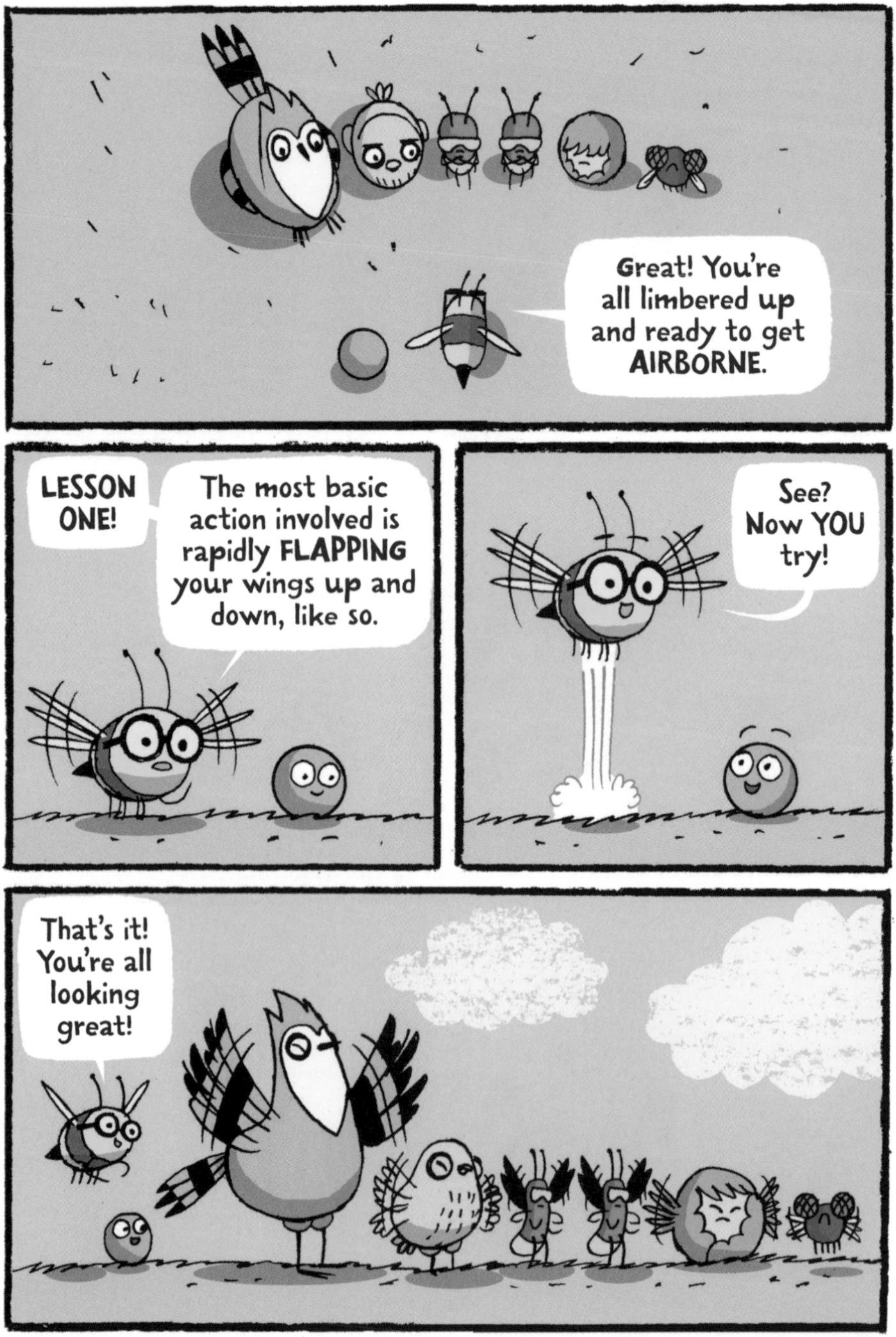

Great! You're all limbered up and ready to get AIRBORNE.
LESSON ONE!
The most basic action involved is rapidly FLAPPING your wings up and down, like so.
See? Now YOU try!
That's it! You're all looking great!

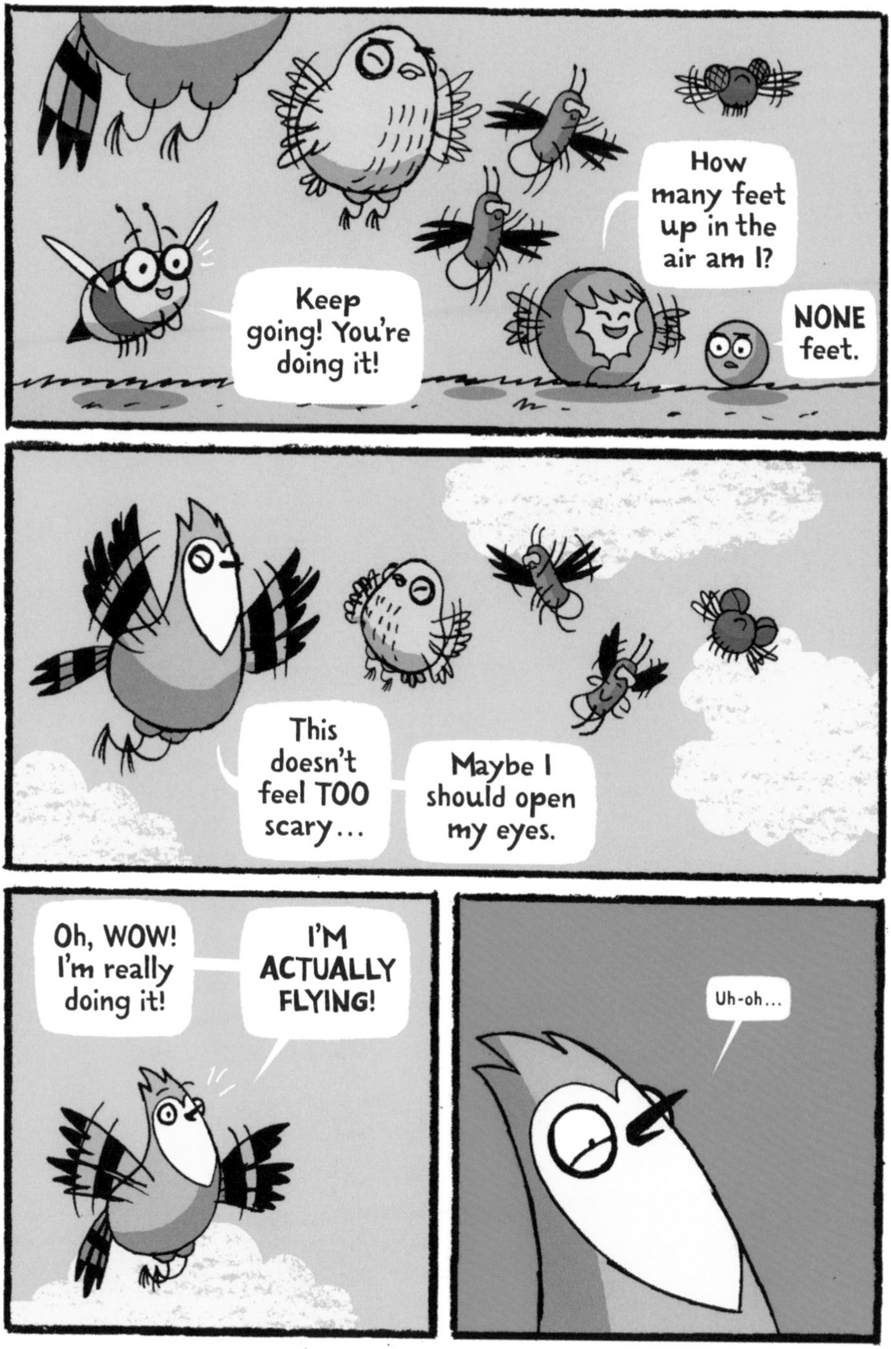
Keep going! You're doing it!
How many feet up in the air am I?
NONE feet.
This doesn't feel TOO scary...
Maybe I should open my eyes.
Oh, WOW! I'm really doing it!
I'M ACTUALLY FLYING!
Uh-oh...

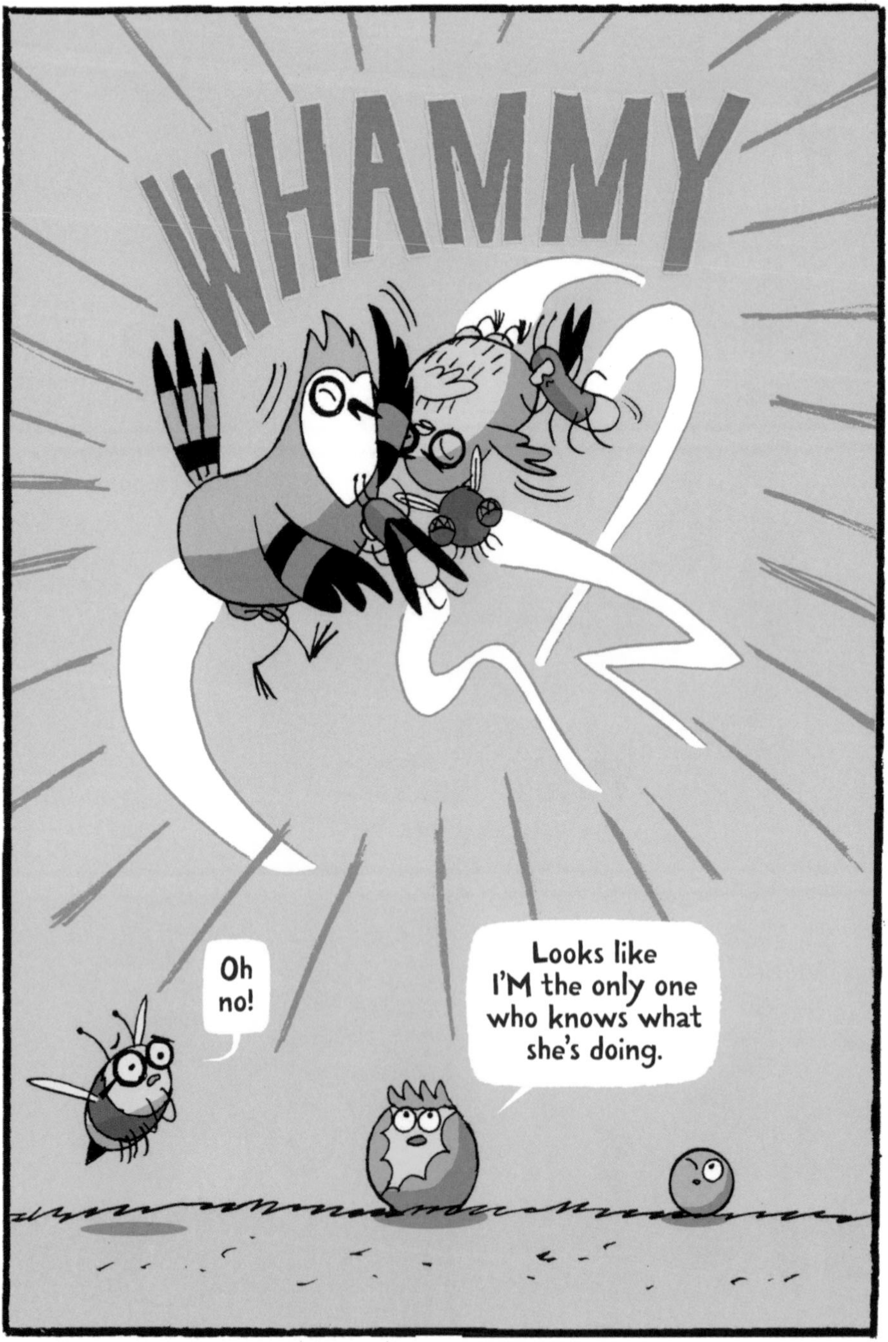
WHAMMY
Oh no!
Looks like I'M the only one who knows what she's doing.

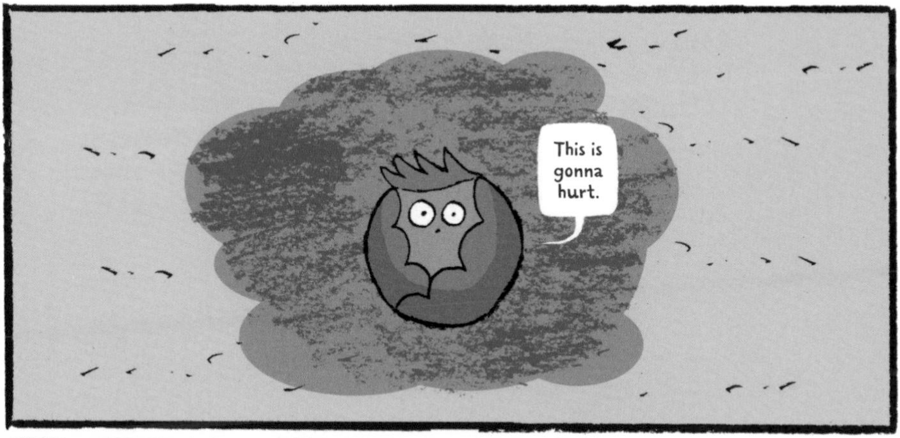
This is gonna hurt.

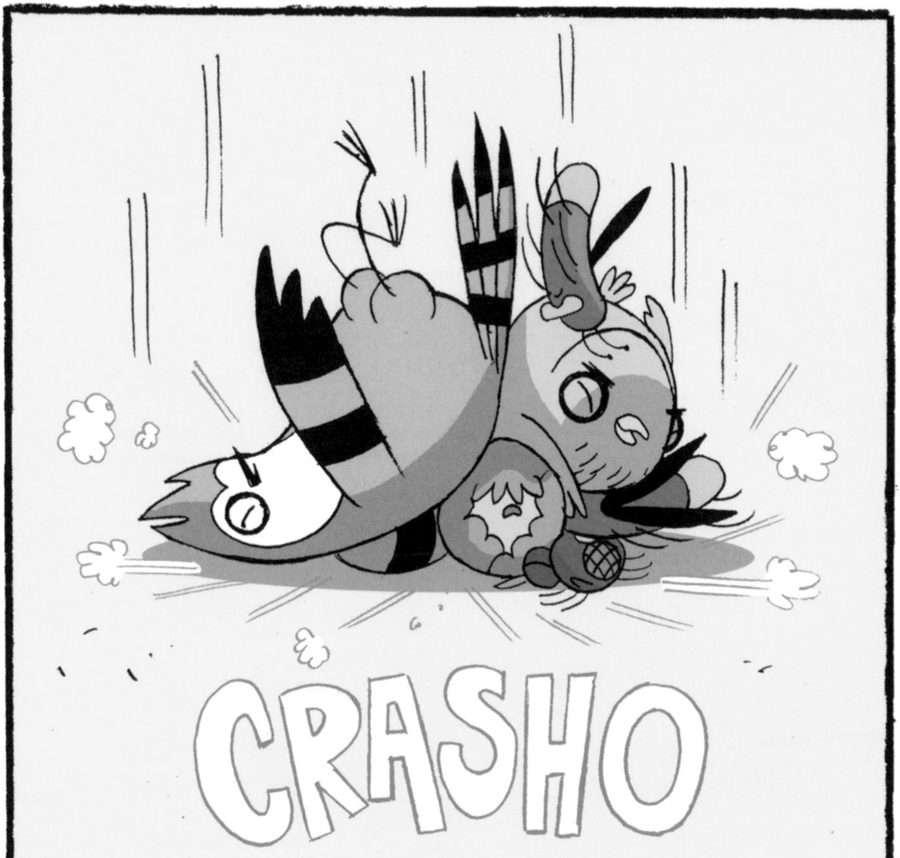
CRASHO

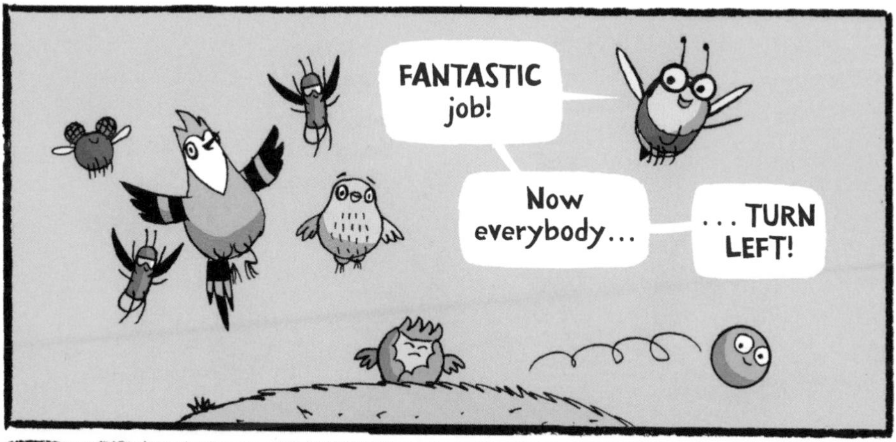
FANTASTIC job!
Now everybody...
...TURN LEFT!

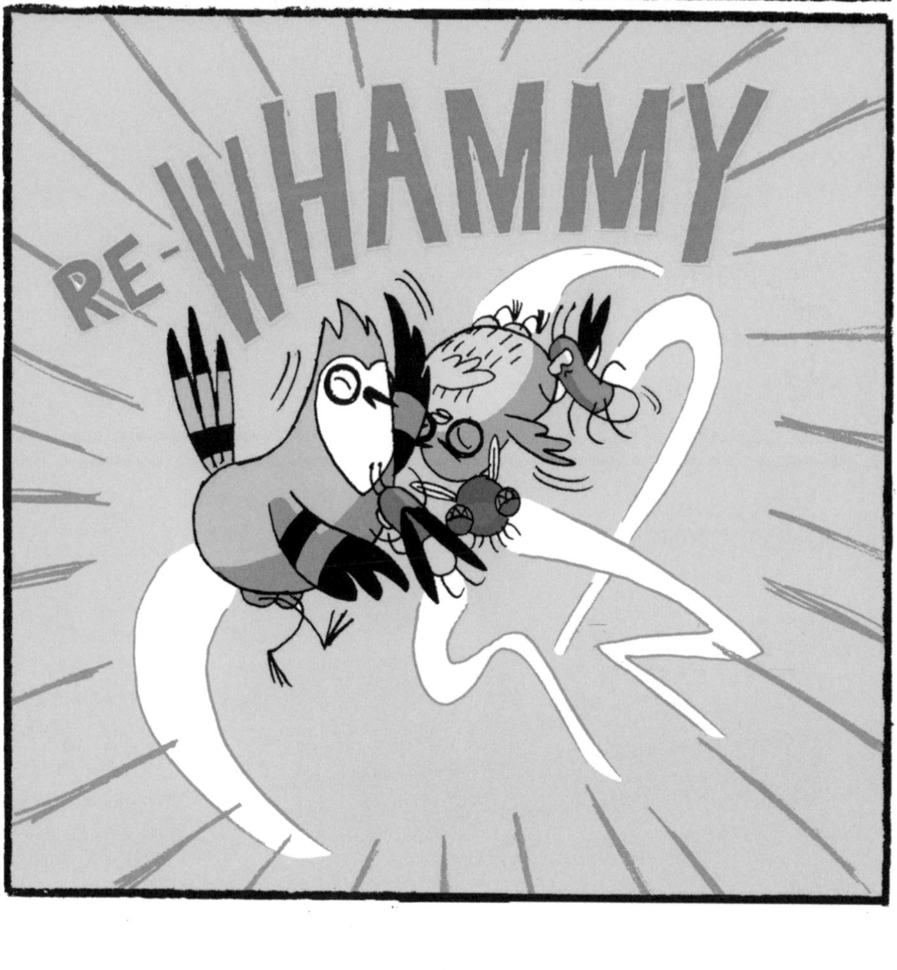
RE-WHAMMY

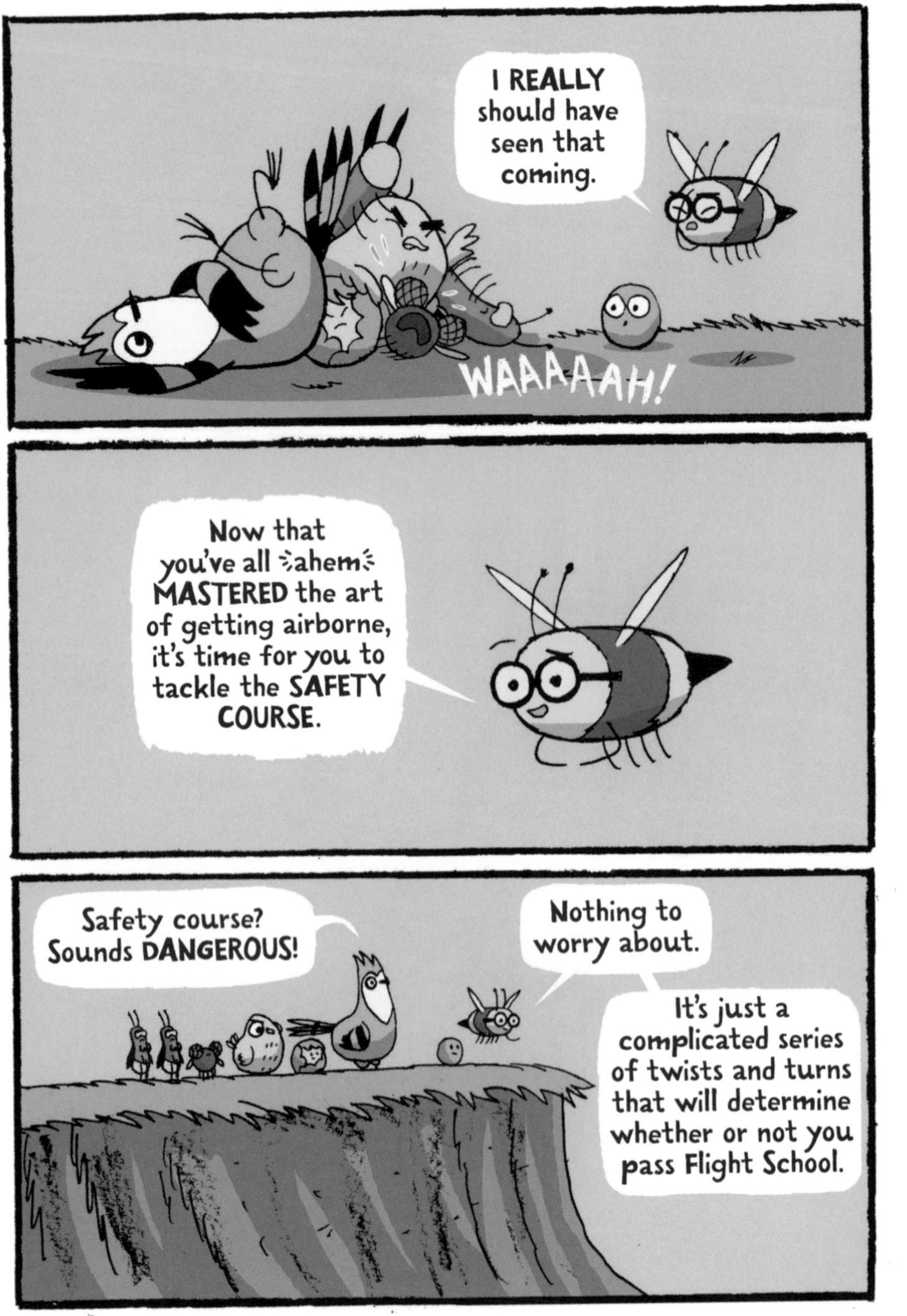
I REALLY should have seen that coming.
WAAAAAH!
Now that you've all ahem MASTERED the art of getting airborne, it's time for you to tackle the SAFETY COURSE.
Safety course? Sounds DANGEROUS!
Nothing to worry about.
It's just a complicated series of twists and turns that will determine whether or not you pass Flight School.

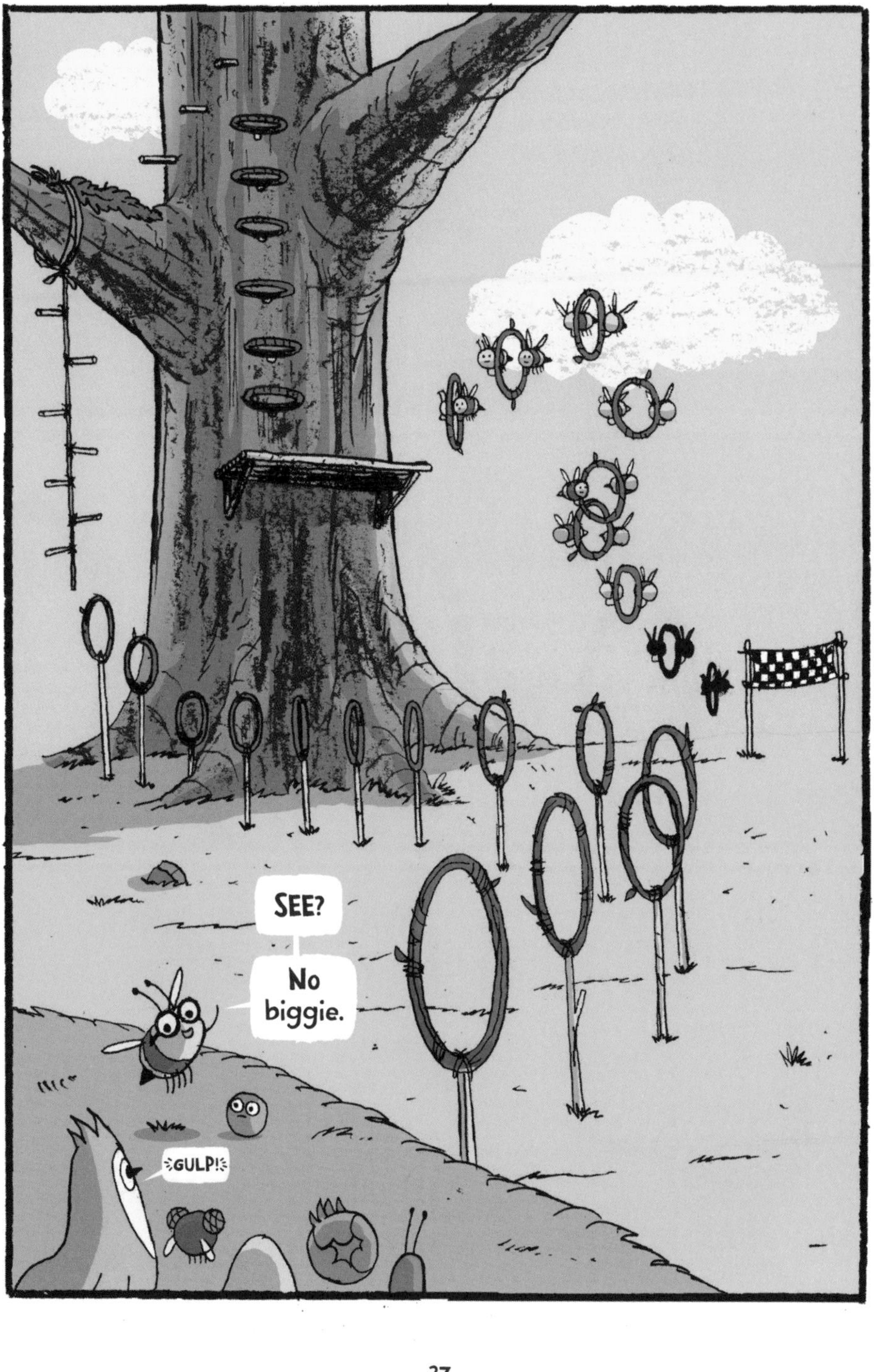
SEE?
No biggie.
GULP!

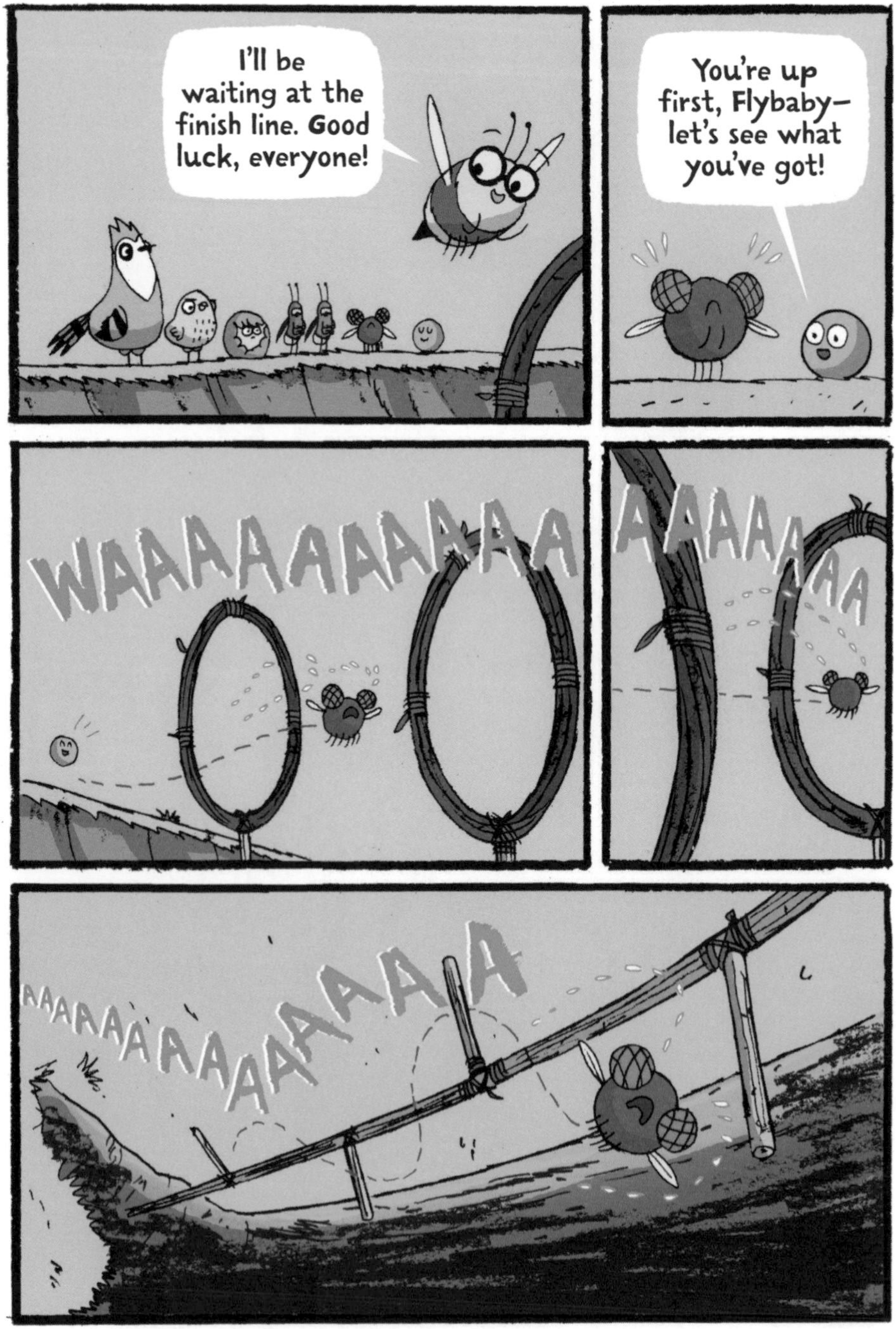
I'll be waiting at the finish line. Good luck, everyone!
You're up first, Flybaby—let's see what you've got!
WAAAAAAAAAAA
AAAAAAAA
AAAAAAAAAAAAAA

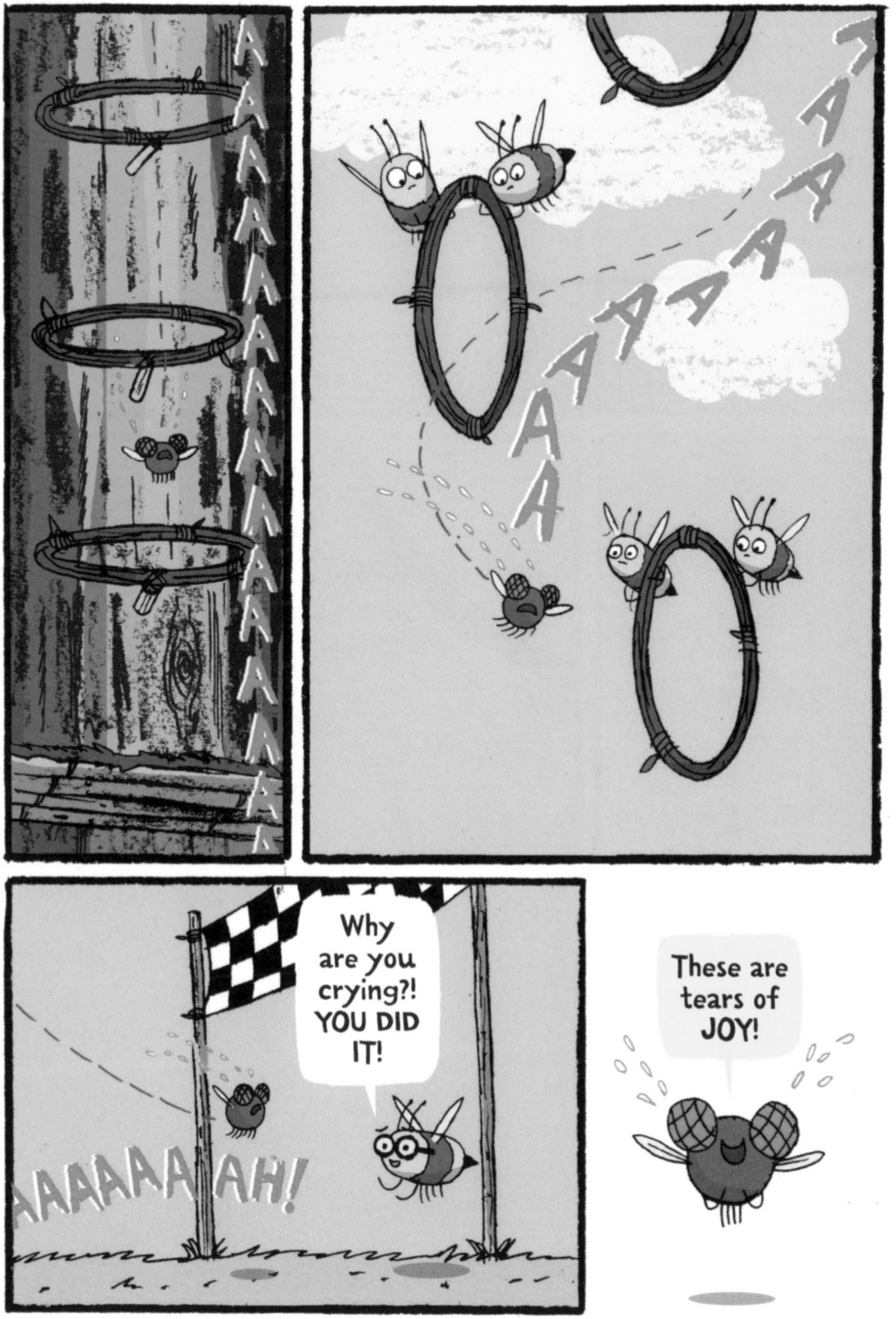
AAAAAAAH!
Why are you crying?! YOU DID IT!
These are tears of JOY!

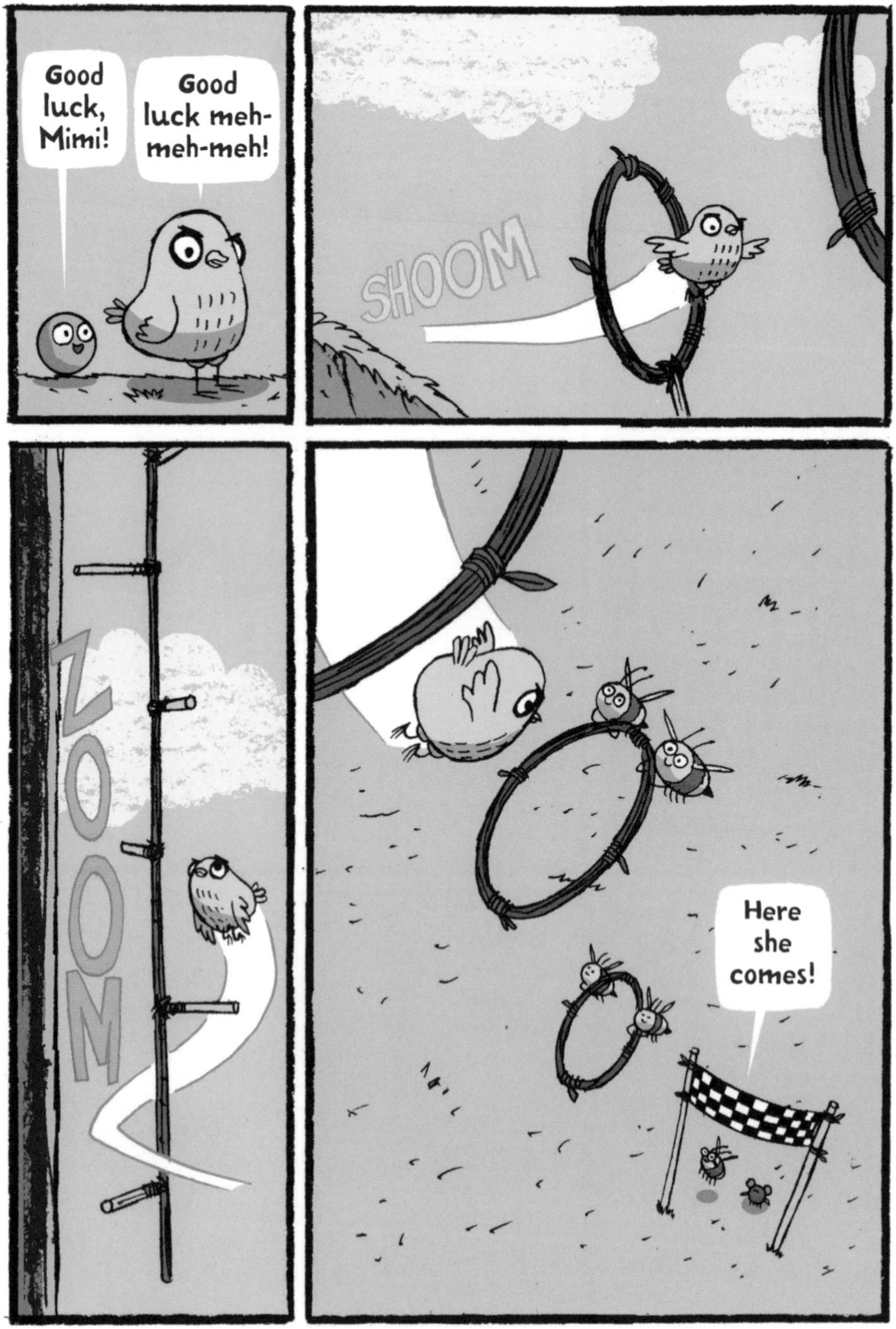
Good luck, Mimi!
Good luck meh-meh-meh!
SHOOM
ZOOM
Here she comes!

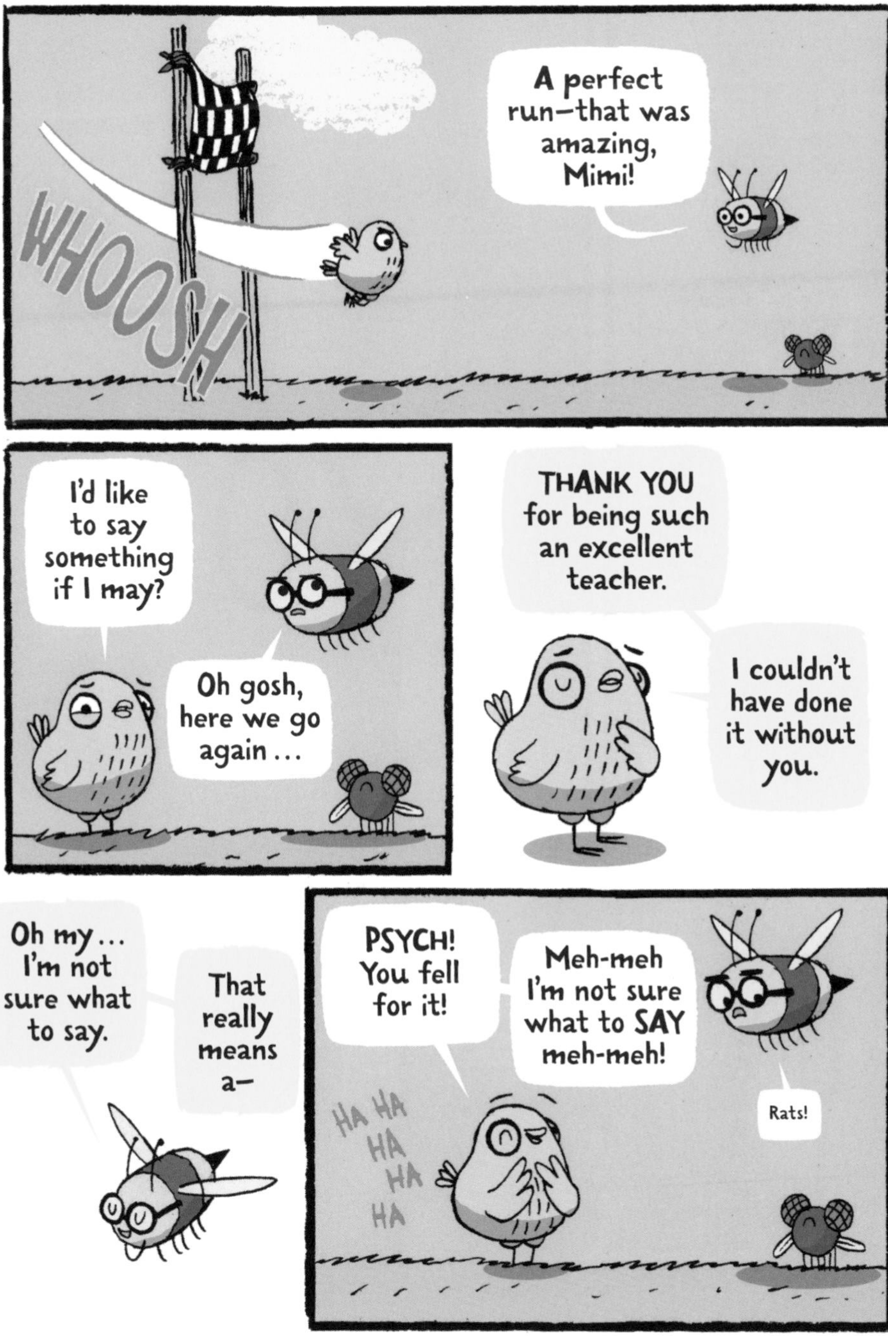
WHOOSH
A perfect run—that was amazing, Mimi!
I'd like to say something if I may?
Oh gosh, here we go again …
THANK YOU for being such an excellent teacher.
I couldn't have done it without you.
Oh my … I'm not sure what to say.
That really means a—
PSYCH! You fell for it!
Meh-meh I'm not sure what to SAY meh-meh!
HA HA HA HA HA HA
Rats!

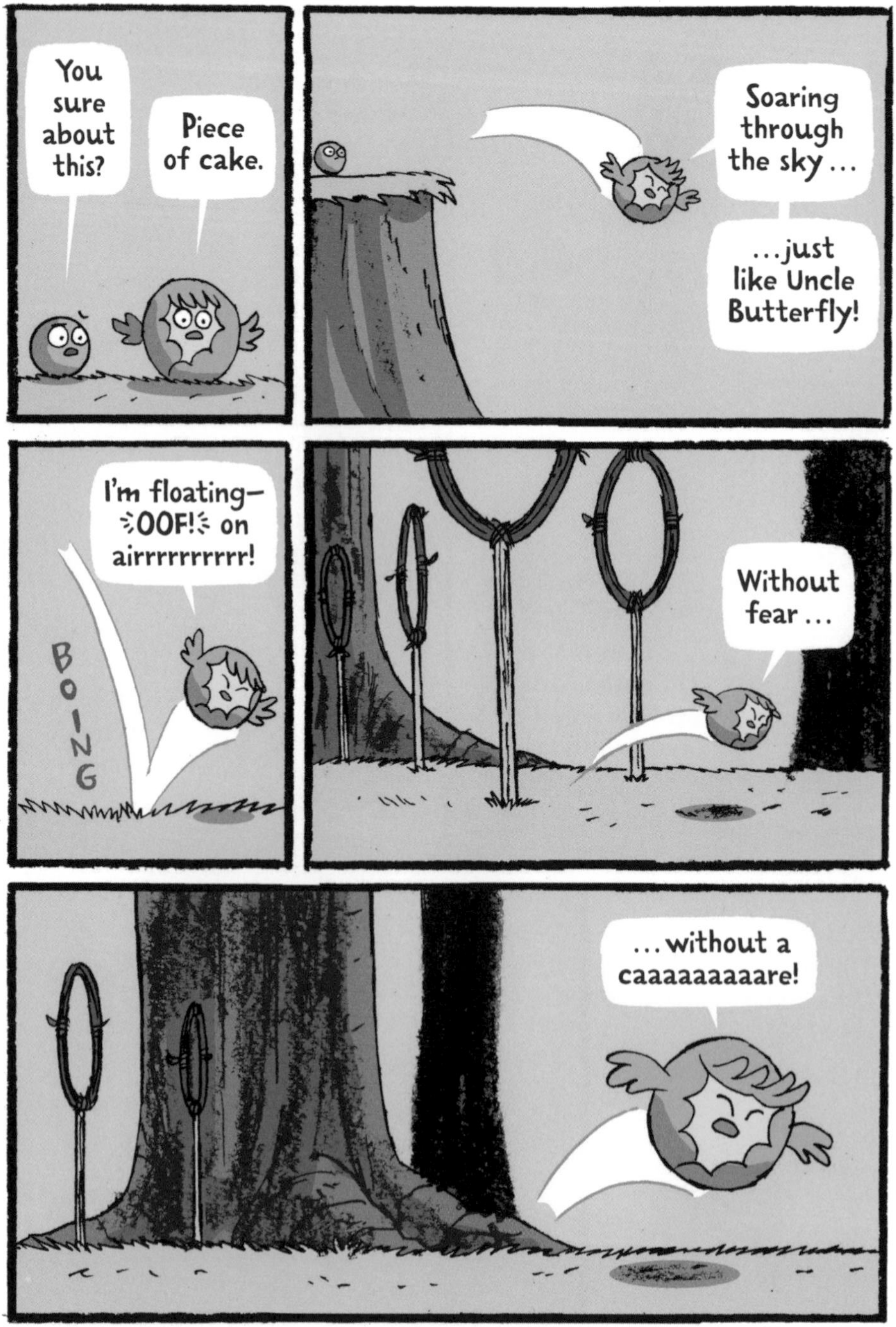
You sure about this?
Piece of cake.
Soaring through the sky...
...just like Uncle Butterfly!
I'm floating— OOF! on airrrrrrrrrr!
BOING
Without fear...
...without a caaaaaaaaare!

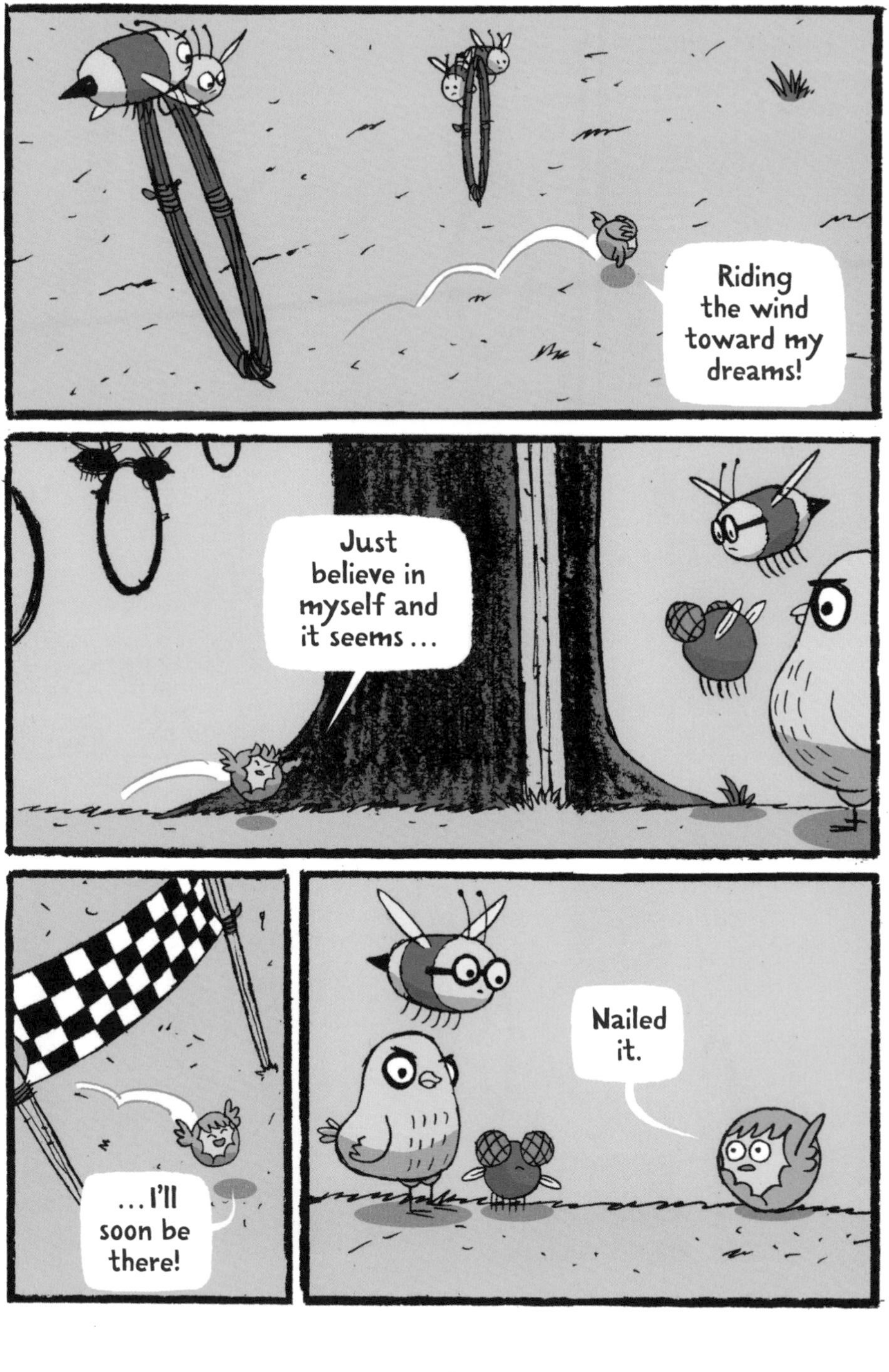
Riding the wind toward my dreams!
Just believe in myself and it seems ...
... I'll soon be there!
Nailed it.

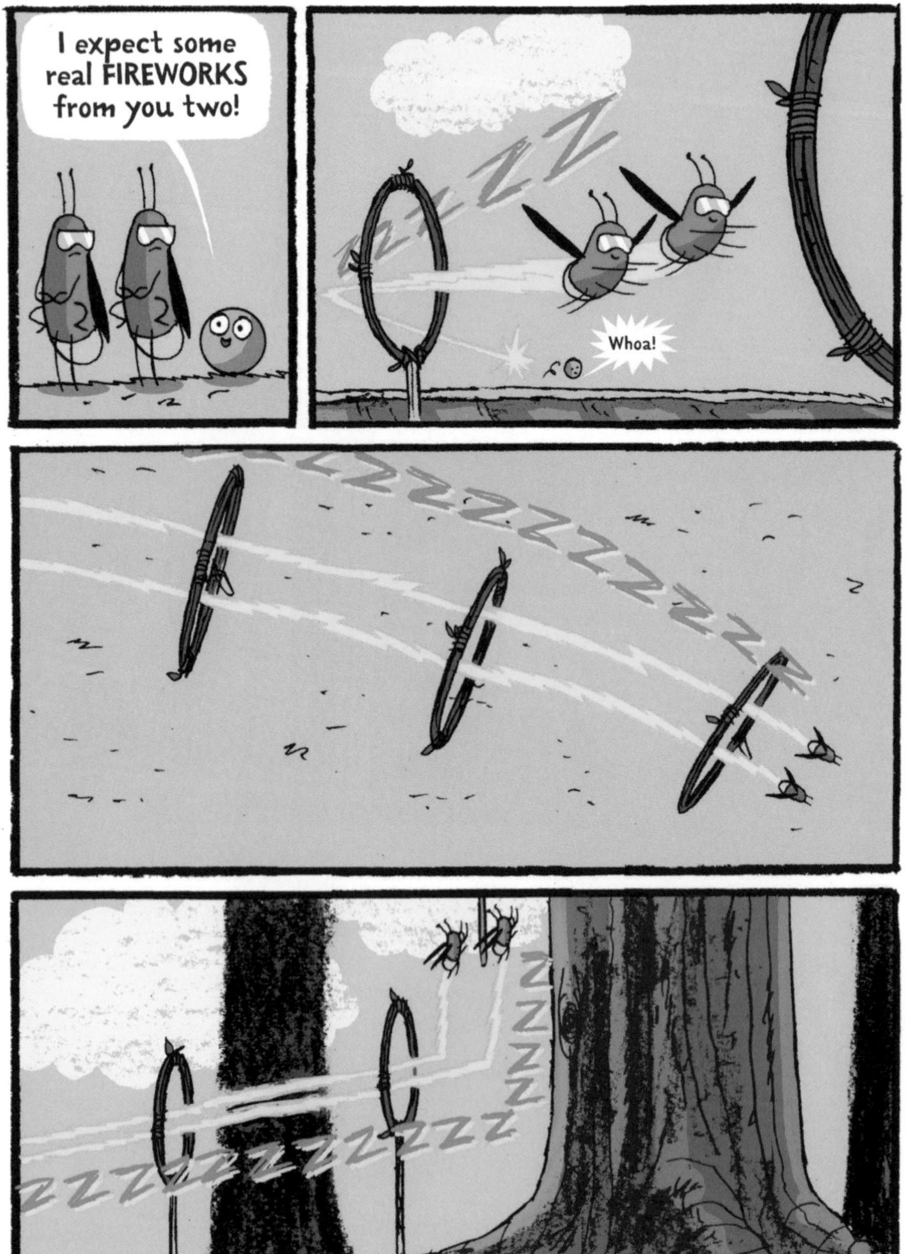
I expect some real FIREWORKS from you two!
Whoa!

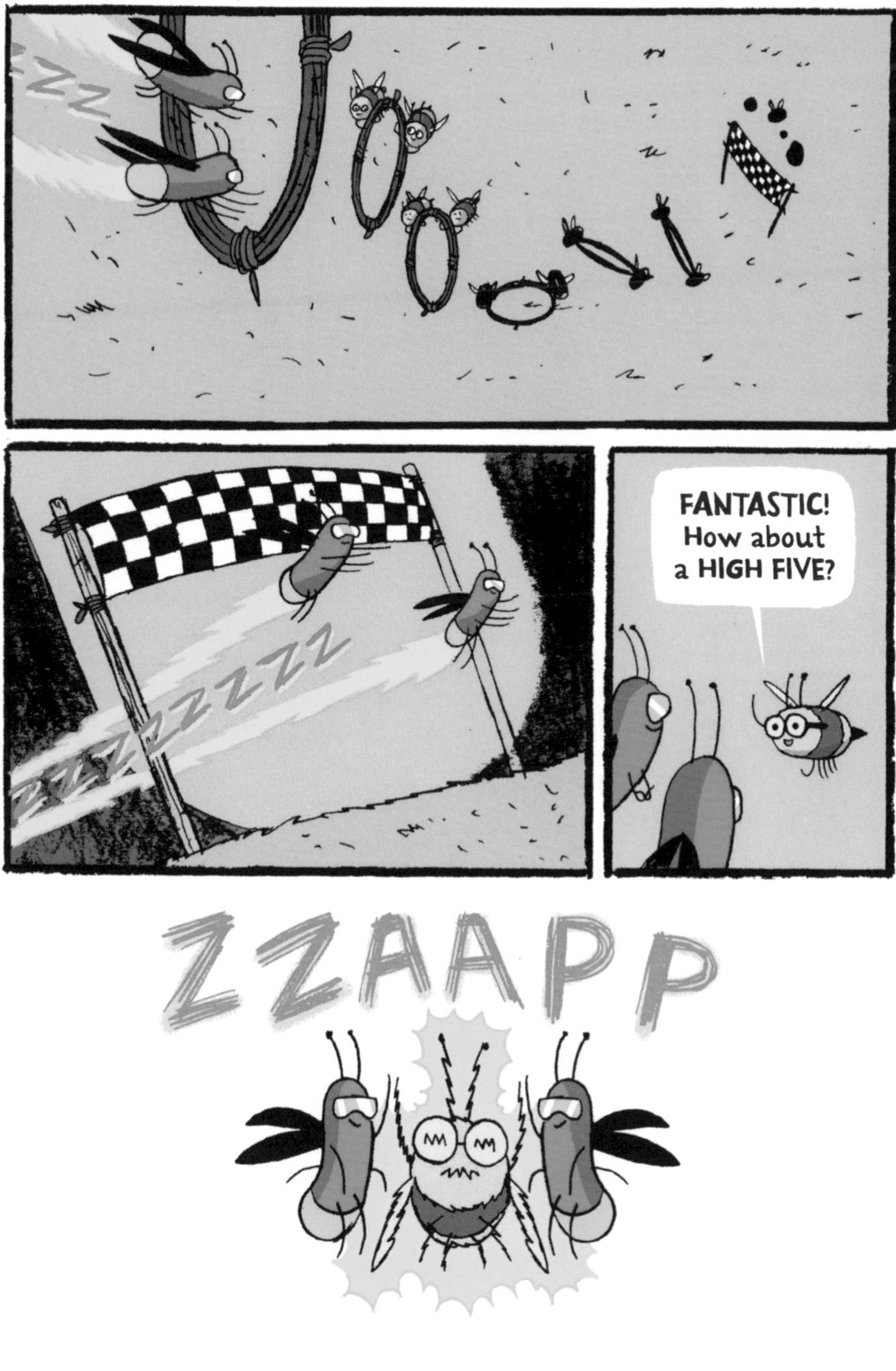
FANTASTIC! How about a HIGH FIVE?
ZZAAPP

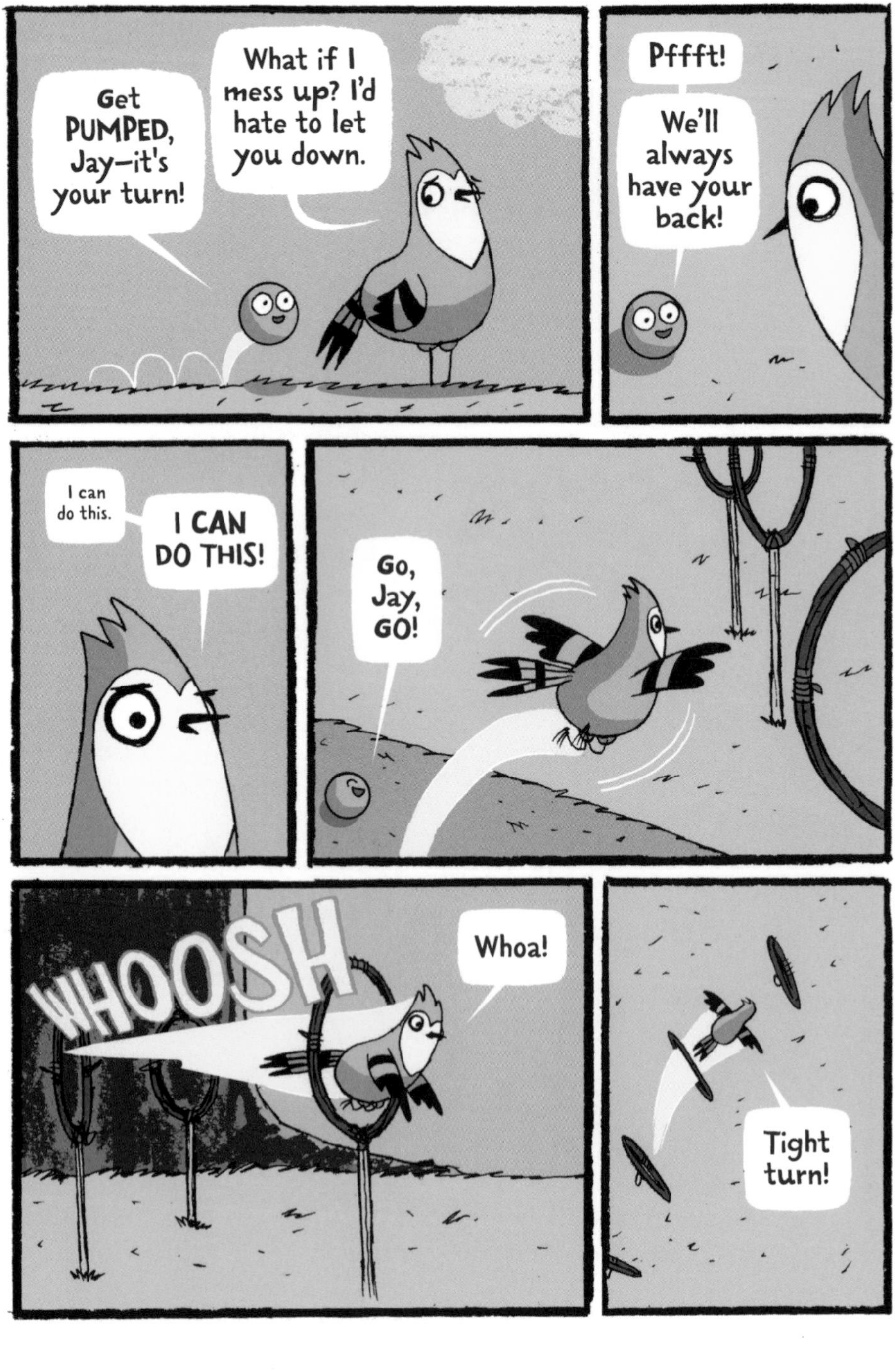
Get PUMPED, Jay—it's your turn!
What if I mess up? I'd hate to let you down.
Pffft!
We'll always have your back!
I can do this.
I CAN DO THIS!
Go, Jay, GO!
WHOOSH
Whoa!
Tight turn!

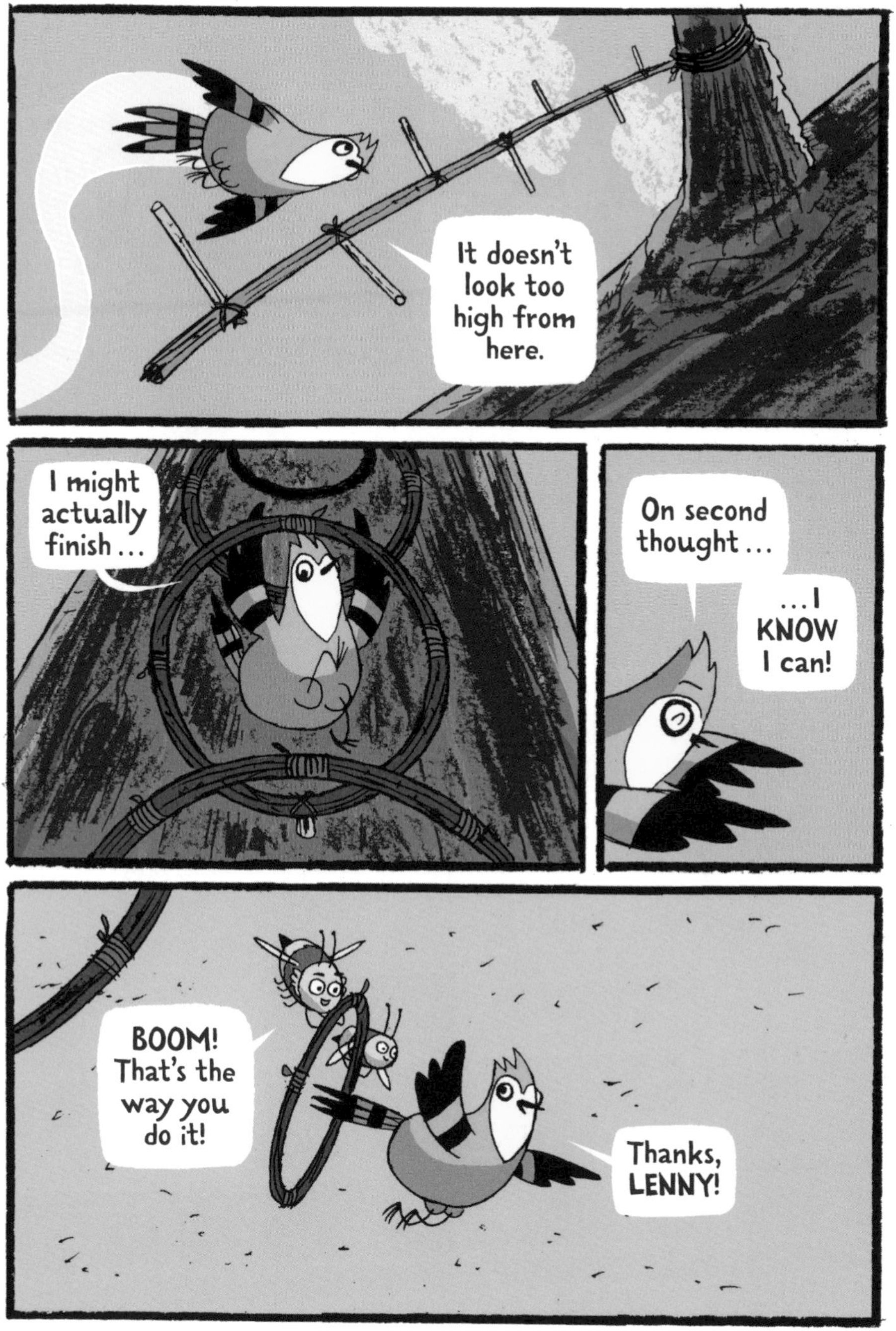
It doesn't look too high from here.
I might actually finish ...
On second thought ...
... I KNOW I can!
BOOM! That's the way you do it!
Thanks, LENNY!

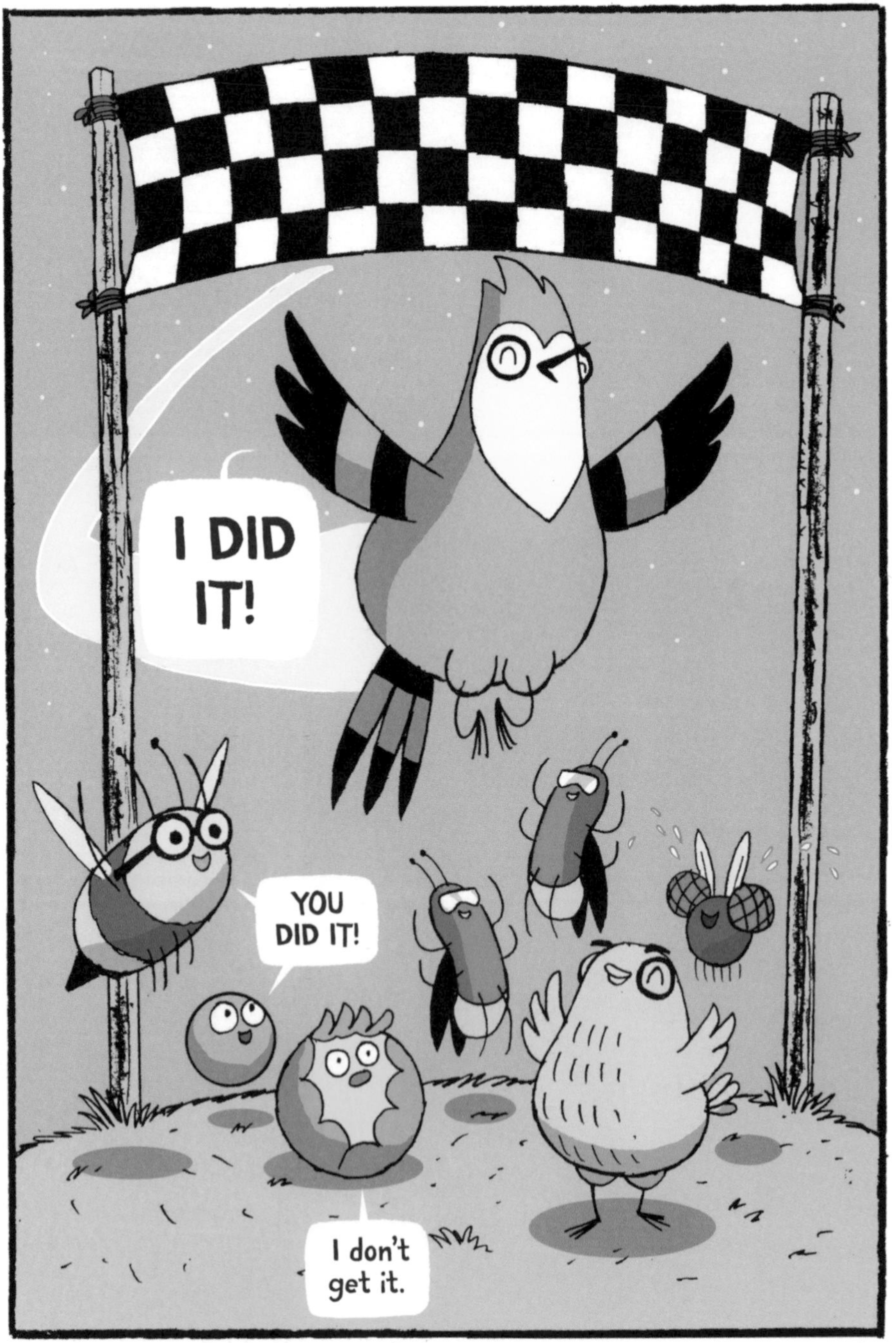
I DID IT!
YOU DID IT!
I don't get it.

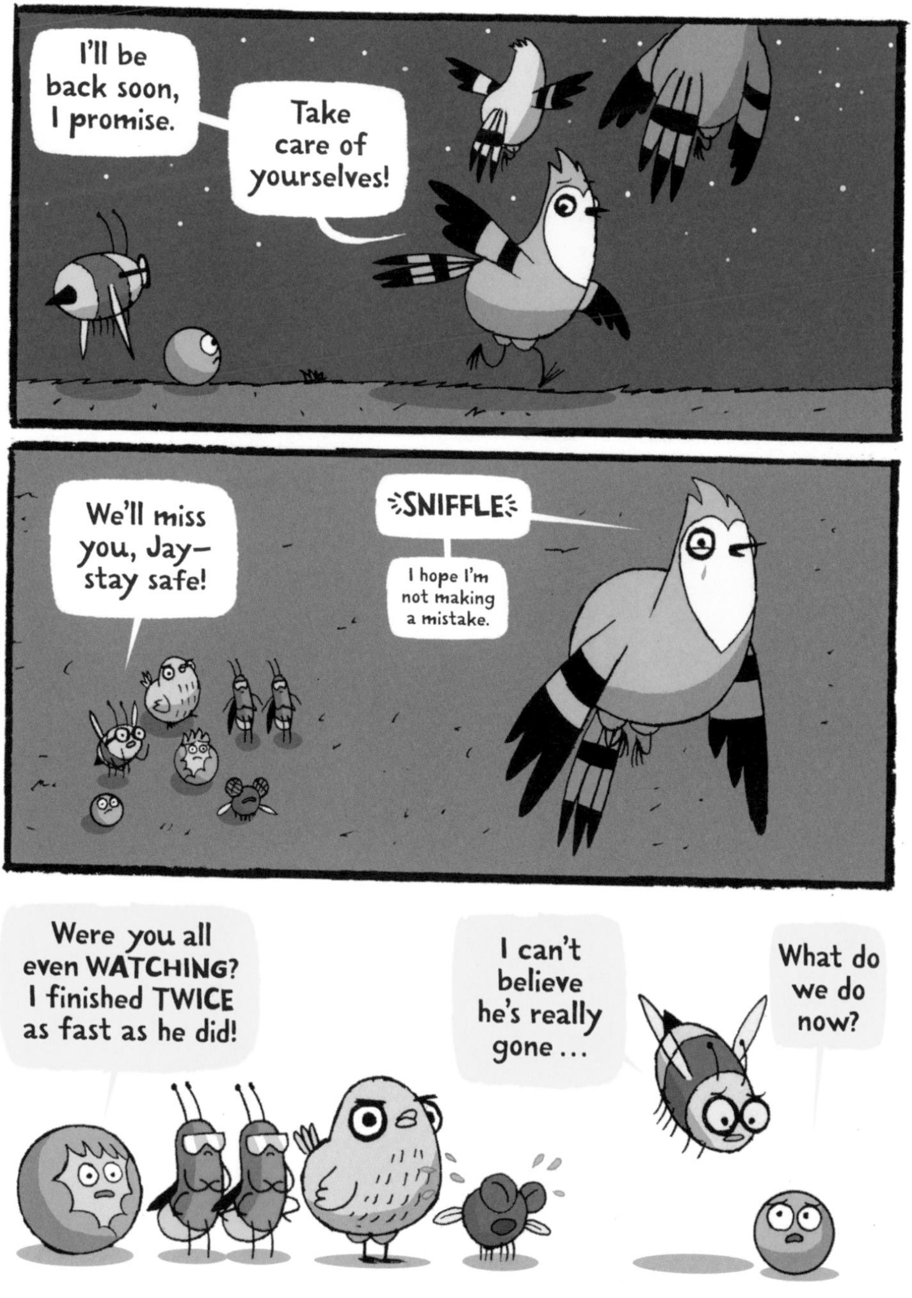
I'll be back soon, I promise.
Take care of yourselves!
We'll miss you, Jay—stay safe!
SNIFFLE
I hope I'm not making a mistake.
Were you all even WATCHING? I finished TWICE as fast as he did!
I can't believe he's really gone . . .
What do we do now?

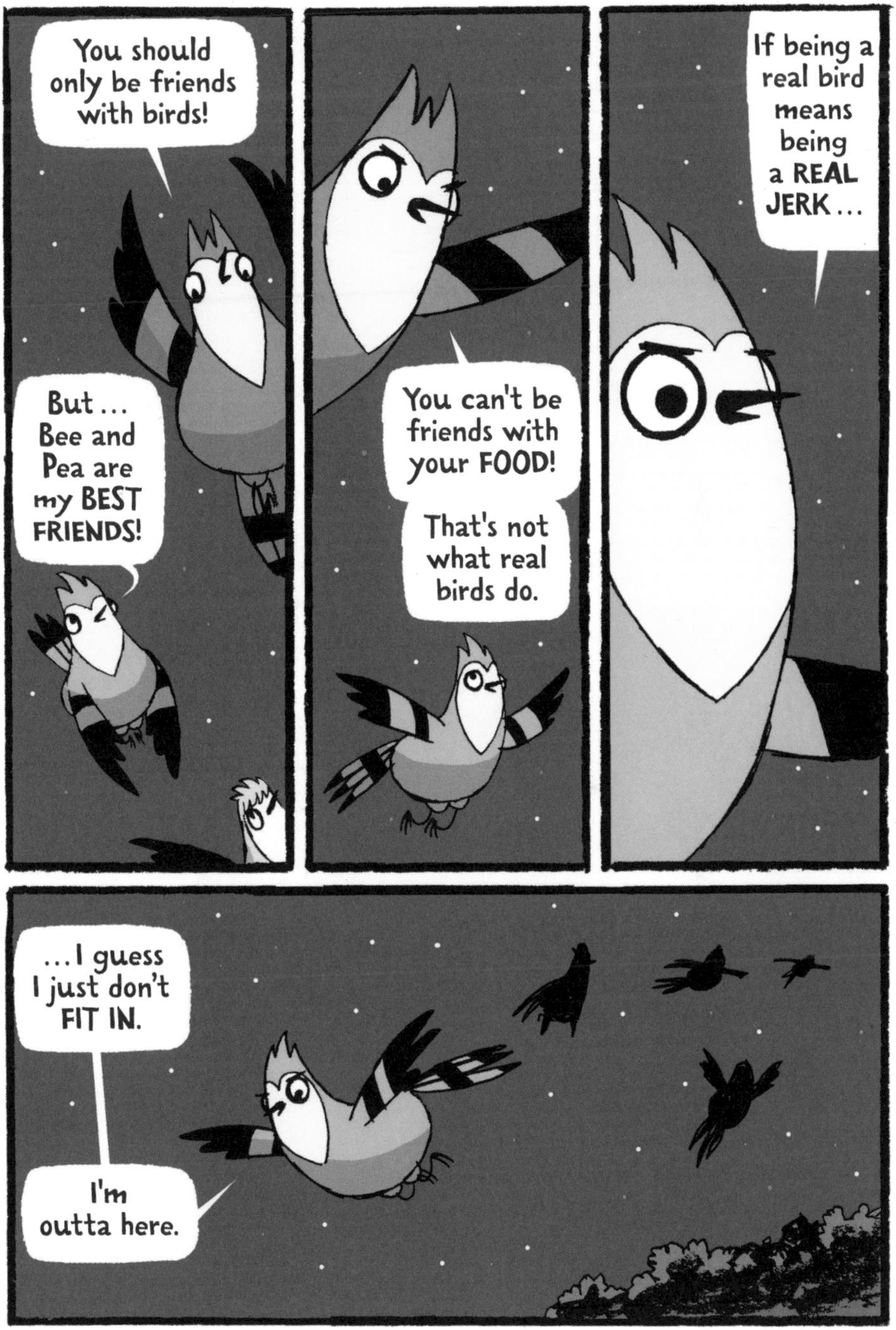

You should only be friends with birds!
But ... Bee and Pea are my BEST FRIENDS!
You can't be friends with your FOOD!
That's not what real birds do.
If being a real bird means being a REAL JERK ...
... I guess I just don't FIT IN.
I'm outta here.

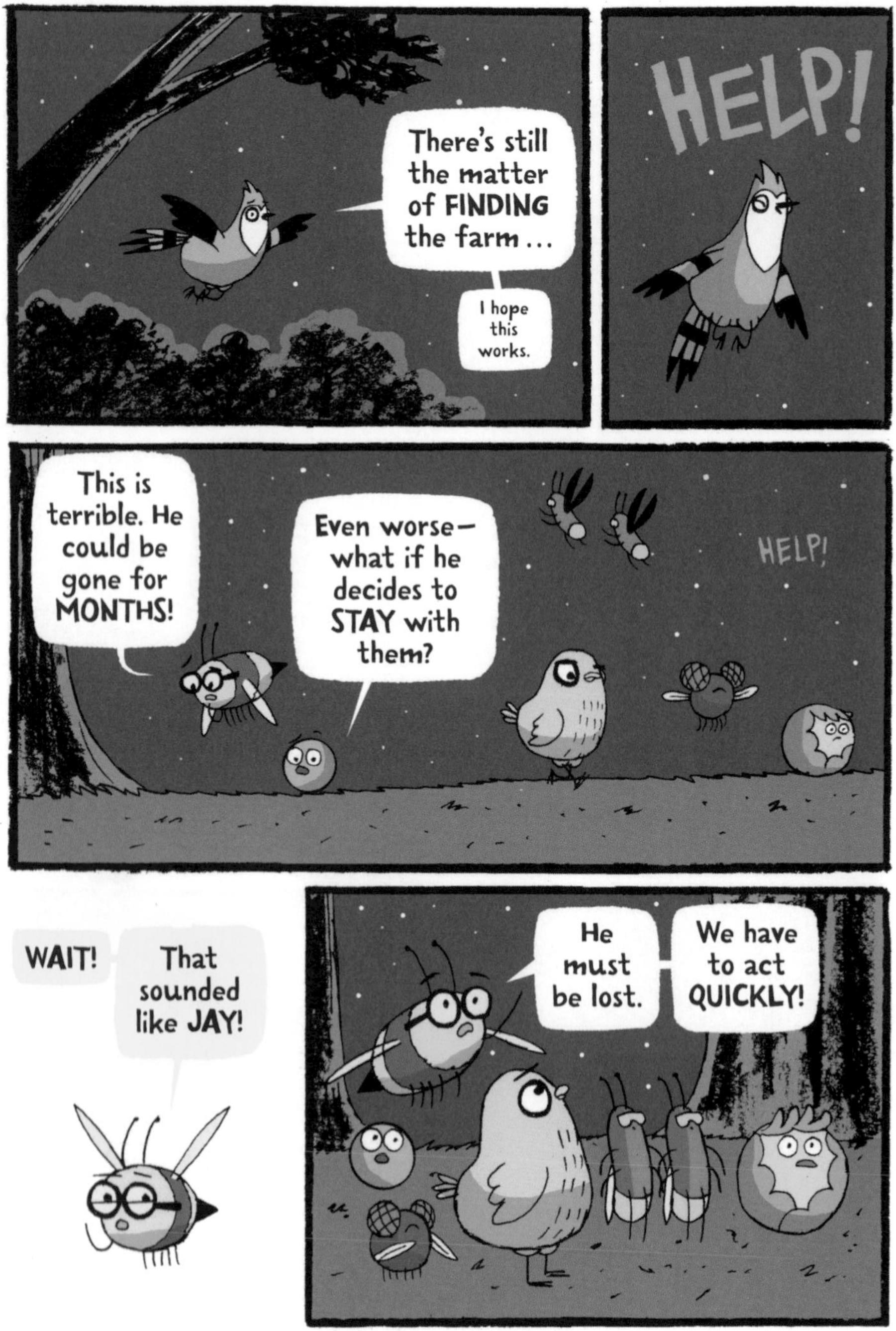
There's still the matter of FINDING the farm...
I hope this works.
HELP!
This is terrible. He could be gone for MONTHS!
Even worse— what if he decides to STAY with them?
HELP!
WAIT!
That sounded like JAY!
He must be lost.
We have to act QUICKLY!

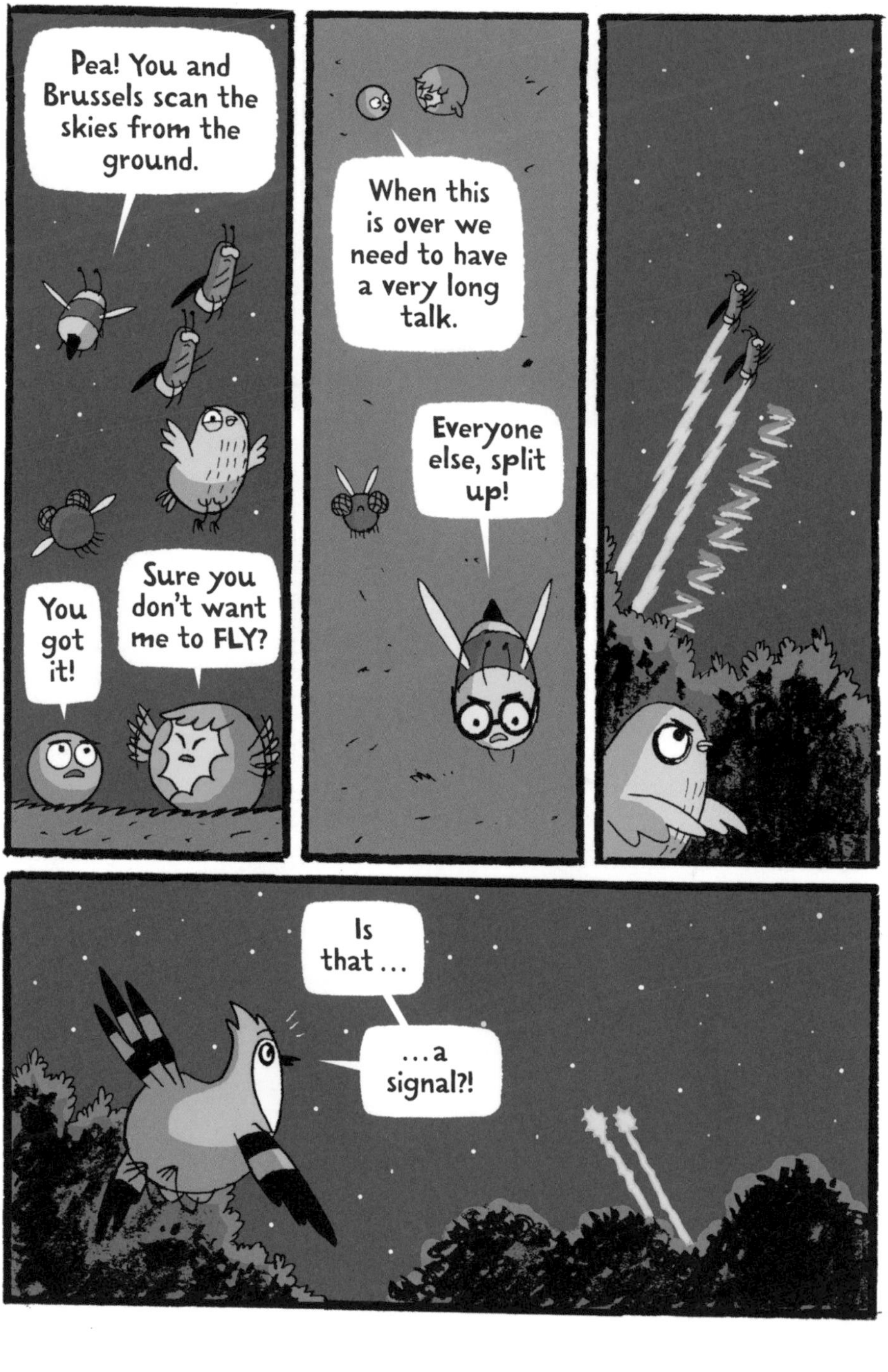

Pea! You and Brussels scan the skies from the ground.
You got it!
Sure you don't want me to FLY?
When this is over we need to have a very long talk.
Everyone else, split up!
Is that . . .
. . . a signal?!

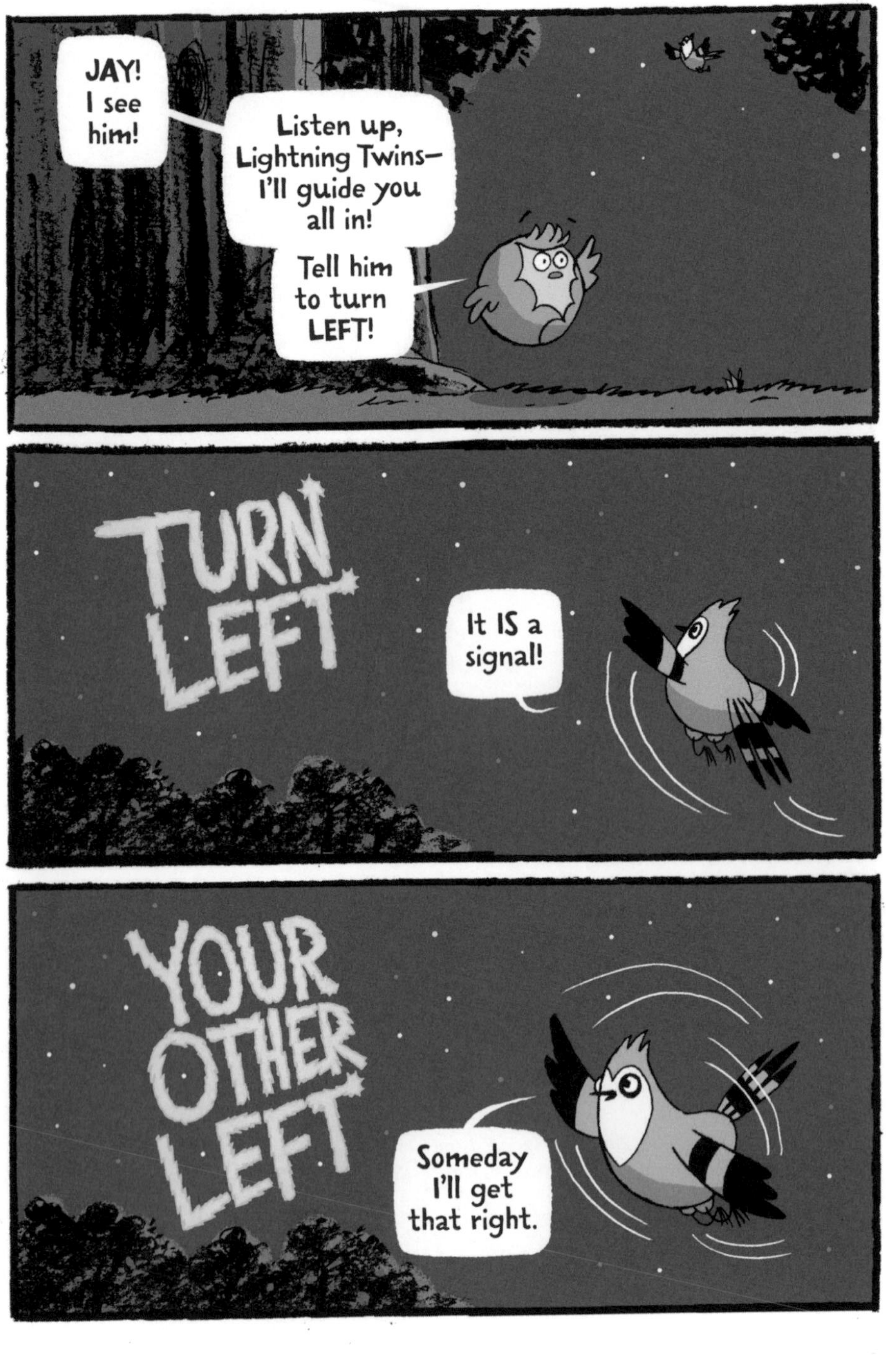
JAY! I see him!
Listen up, Lightning Twins— I'll guide you all in!
Tell him to turn LEFT!
TURN LEFT
It IS a signal!
YOUR OTHER LEFT
Someday I'll get that right.

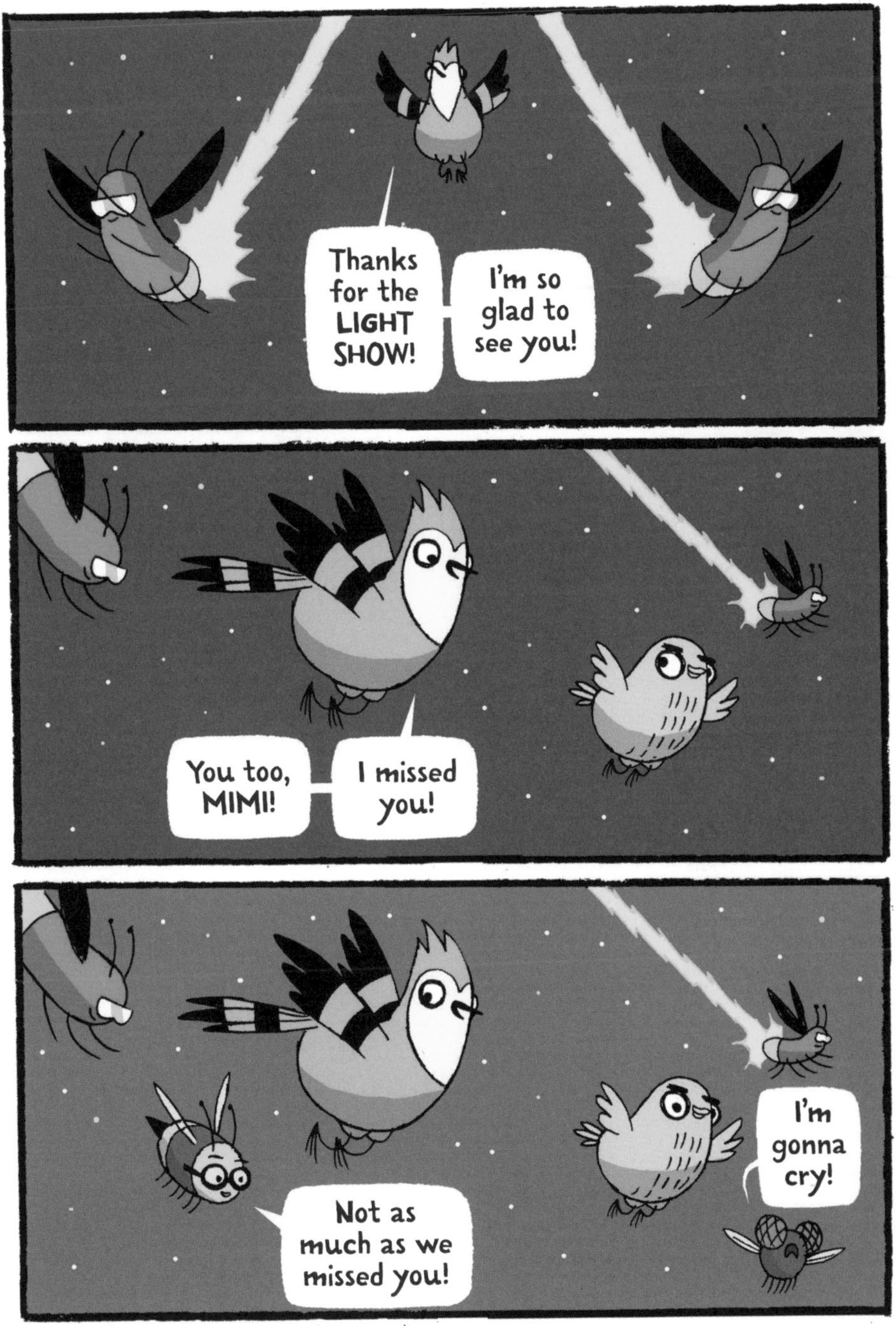
Thanks for the LIGHT SHOW!
I'm so glad to see you!
You too, MIMI!
I missed you!
Not as much as we missed you!
I'm gonna cry!